DR DEVEREUX'S PROPOSAL

BY
MARGARET McDONAGH

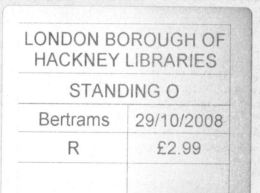

MILLS & BOON®
Pure reading pleasure™

First published in Great Britain 2008
Harlequin Mills & Boon Limited,
Eton House, 18-24 Paradise Road, Richmond, Surrey TW9 1SR

© Margaret McDonagh 2008

ISBN: 978 0 263 86356 7

Set in Times Roman 10½ on 12 pt
03-1108-56027

Printed and bound in Spain
by Litografia Rosés, S.A., Barcelona

Margaret McDonagh says of herself: 'I began losing myself in the magical world of books from a very young age, and I always knew that I had to write, pursuing the dream for over twenty years, often with cussed stubbornness in the face of rejection letters! Despite having numerous romance novellas, short stories and serials published, the news that my first "proper book" had been accepted by Harlequin Mills & Boon for their Medical™ Romance line brought indescribable joy! Having a passion for learning makes researching an involving pleasure, and I love developing new characters, getting to know them, setting them challenges to overcome. The hardest part is saying goodbye to them, because they become so real to me. And I always fall in love with my heroes! Writing and reading books, keeping in touch with friends, watching sport and meeting the demands of my four-legged companions keeps me well occupied. I hope you enjoy reading this book as much as I loved writing it.'

www.margaretmcdonagh.com

margaret.mcdonagh@yahoo.co.uk

With special thanks...

To those who helped with my research on retinitis
pigmentosa...your courage is humbling
www.brps.org.uk...
and on Duchenne muscular dystrophy
www.muscular-dystrophy.org

To my fellow Medical Romance authors
involved in this exciting series

And to the wonderful editorial team who conceived the
Penhally project—thank you for believing in me.

BRIDES OF PENHALLY BAY

*Bachelor doctors become husbands and fathers—
in a place where hearts are made whole.*

**At Christmas we met pregnant doctor Lucy Tremayne
when she was reunited with the man she loves**
Christmas Eve Baby by Caroline Anderson

**Then in January we snuggled up for some much needed
winter warmth with gorgeous Italian doctor Marco Avanti**
The Italian's New-Year Marriage Wish by Sarah Morgan

**February saw Adam and Maggie on a 24-hour rescue
mission where romance blossomed as the sun started to set**
The Doctor's Bride By Sunrise by Josie Metcalfe

**Single dad Jack Tremayne found a mother
for his little boy—and a bride for himself in March**
The Surgeon's Fatherhood Surprise by Jennifer Taylor

**A princess arrived in Penhally when
HRH Melinda Fortesque came to the Bay in April**
The Doctor's Royal Love-Child by Kate Hardy

In May Edward Tremayne found the woman of his dreams
Nurse Bride, Bayside Wedding by Gill Sanderson

**Hunky Penhally Bay Chief Inspector Lachlan D'Ancey
found love in June**
Single Dad Seeks a Wife by Melanie Milburne

**The temperature really hotted up in July, when devastatingly
handsome Dr Oliver Fawkner arrived in the Bay…**
Virgin Midwife, Playboy Doctor by Margaret McDonagh

**In August, Francesca and Mike
tried one last time for the baby they'd always longed for…**
Their Miracle Baby by Caroline Anderson

**September brought sexy Sheikh Zayed from his
desert kingdom to the beaches of Penhally**
Sheikh Surgeon Claims His Bride by Josie Metcalfe

We snuggled up with dishy Dr Tom Cornish in October
A Baby for Eve by Maggie Kingsley

And this month French doctor Gabriel sweeps into the Bay!
Dr Devereux's Proposal by Margaret McDonagh

A collection to treasure for ever!

CHAPTER ONE

'QUE L'ENFER?' Shocked by the sight that greeted him as his destination came into view, Dr Gabriel Devereux drew his car to a halt at the side of the cliff road and stepped out. *'Mon Dieu!'*

What had happened to the small Cornish town of Penhally Bay? His one previous visit had been in the summer when he had spent a weekend looking around and finalising details for his year-long contract to work as a GP in the local practice. Penhally had recently been twinned with St Ouen-sur-Mer in Normandy, France, where he had been filling in for the last ten months at his friend François Amiot's busy medical clinic.

As part of the twinning process, people from different occupations and ways of life were crossing the Channel, exchanging jobs and skills, building bridges and friendships, bringing the communities of the two towns together, socially, commercially and culturally. None of the other doctors in St Ouen-sur-Mer had been prepared to move their families for a year, but for Gabriel it had been too good an opportunity to miss. Taking this post in Cornwall was a heaven-sent chance to put even more distance between himself and the unresolved issues that had seen him leave Paris for St Ouen-sur-Mer in the first place.

Ruthlessly banishing any thoughts of home, Gabriel's gaze narrowed as he concentrated on the scene of devastation below him. In the summer, Penhally Bay had been an attractive, hilly, seaside town bustling with tourists and basking under sunshine and clear blue skies. The rows of houses, shops and businesses along the curving seafront, painted in an array of pastel colours, had watched over the boats that had bobbed gently in the harbour. Now… He shook his head in disbelief. This cloudy late October day, the scene could not have been more different.

When his new boss, Nick Tremayne, the senior partner at the Penhally practice, had emailed a week ago to confirm the date to begin work, he had mentioned a flash flood, but Gabriel had not fully grasped the seriousness of what had occurred. A man of few words, Nick had not gone into detail, but Gabriel could see that the event had been far more cataclysmic than that one brief email had implied.

After breathing in a lungful of fresh, salty, Cornish air, Gabriel climbed back in the car and drove down the hill to the town. He passed the promontory on which the church and the lighthouse stood, before heading along the seafront that formed a horseshoe round the harbour. At the far western end of the arc were the lifeboat station and the surgery where he would be working from Monday. Halfway around the seafront, he slowed as he neared the bridge. Here, the river Lanson, which flowed down the hill between Bridge Street and Gull Close, effectively cutting the town in two, spilled its waters into the harbour.

This central area appeared to have borne the brunt of the flooding with damage obvious to houses in Bridge Street and around the seafront. The end wall of the Anchor Hotel—on the corner of Gull Close and Harbour Road—had come down under the force of the water. Standing forlorn and closed for business, the remains of the building were shored up with scaffolding, and demolition notices warned that the property was unsafe.

Twelve days on, the waters had receded and the clean-up operation had begun, but the empty houses and shops were all too apparent, as was the debris that had washed down the angry river in full spate. Ruined and discarded belongings sat forlornly outside abandoned properties, full skips awaited collection and disposal, while redundant sandbags remained by doors and gateways.

The town bustled with life, however. These people clearly had spirit, banding together and refusing to allow the difficult circumstances to defeat them. It was past lunchtime and the Saturday market was thriving. People were shopping in the stores that had evaded damage, a few were fishing off the harbour wall or working on their boats, while dedicated parties were continuing the task of restoring order after the flood. Gabriel planned to do all he could to help in the days and weeks ahead…but first he needed to find the house that was to be his base for the next year, move in and find his feet.

As he reached the outskirts of town, his memory guiding him down a narrow, hedge-lined lane, he experienced a flicker of uncharacteristic nervousness. He hoped he would settle here, that he would be accepted…a stranger and a foreigner in this tight community. Penhally Bay was not the cosmopolitan metropolis of London where he had spent time during his medical training. Would the people here judge him on his skills as a doctor or on being different? He hoped the former…was wary of the latter.

Half a mile farther along the lane, he came to the turning he was seeking and steered the car between the twin gateposts that marked the unpaved driveway. To one side was Gatehouse Cottage, the single-storey thatched lodge which Nick Tremayne had told him belonged to the physiotherapist at the surgery. Gabriel frowned, unable to remember her name. There were no signs of life from the cottage so he hoped his arrival had gone unnoticed. The drive curved away from the lodge and fifty yards farther on the impressive but not-too-large Manor House came into view, sheltered and surrounded by mature shrubs and trees. Gabriel paused, admiring the traditional fifteenth-century building, feeling now the same contentment he had experienced when he had first been here in late July.

Symbolically, the clouds overhead cleared, and low autumn sunshine filtered down from a patch of pale blue sky, highlighting myriad colours in the old, lichen-spotted granite blocks and dark roof slates from which the Manor House was built. Instinct told him he had been right to come here. This was what he needed. A place where he could work with his customary enthusiasm for the job he loved…a refuge where he could be alone and decide what he was going to do about the rest of his life.

He parked his car at the rear of the building, out of sight should anyone approach up the drive. He had arrived a day early and planned to take time to himself before announcing his presence. After finding the keys to the house—left for him by the solicitor acting for the owners, who were working abroad long term—he collected together his essential belongings and let himself in. He knew the house had been empty since the last tenants had departed at the end of August, so he was surprised to find the air smelling fresh and the surfaces clean of dust. Someone had been thoughtful enough to make preparations for his arrival. The knowledge warmed him.

Upstairs, he selected a bedroom with a lovely view over the surrounding countryside. Whoever had taken care of the house had anticipated his choice, because clean linen was folded neatly on the huge four-poster bed and fresh towels were hanging on the heated rail in the *en suite* bathroom. Bars of unfussy, masculine soap, still in their wrappers, sat on the basin and in the generous shower cubicle. Appreciating the welcoming touches, and making a mental note to discover the identity of and thank the unknown cleaner, Gabriel stripped off his clothes and headed for the shower.

Hot water jetted down, easing the kinks out of his body, soothing his muscles and restoring his jaded spirit, making him realise how much tension remained coiled inside him.

'You're sure this is what you want?' François had asked him as he had come to see him off the day before. 'I don't want you to feel obligated to go to Cornwall because none of the rest of us are willing to uproot ourselves.'

'It's not that,' Gabriel had reassured his friend.

Frowning, François had helped him load his bags into the car. 'You're worried about interference from home?'

'Always.' His smile had been wry, hiding the inner turmoil that had plagued him for months. 'I need the distance, the space to make some decisions.'

'You know I'll watch your back. I won't be giving out details of your whereabouts to anyone. Especially now we know what Yvette is capable of to achieve her ends.'

Gabriel had nodded in gratitude. 'Thanks, *mon ami*. But you and I will keep in touch.'

'Try to get rid of me! I want regular texts and emails.'

He would miss François and his wife, having stayed with the couple for the last ten months. 'You and Celeste take care.'

'We will—and we really appreciate the way you stepped in when we needed you,' Francois had told him.

'That's what friends are for.'

After shaking hands and exchanging a brief hug, Gabriel had driven away from St Ouen-sur-Mer filled with nervous anticipation for what lay ahead. One chapter was over—a new one was about to begin.

Now, remembering that conversation, he closed his eyes and tipped his face to the shower spray. Today was the first day of the rest of his life. It was up to him what he made of it…whether he went his own way or allowed old ghosts and new pressures to trap him into something he knew he didn't want. This posting to Cornwall had bought him some extra time. Time he intended to use wisely, making the decisions that would set the course of his future.

Shutting off the water, he stepped out of the cubicle and reached for a towel, hesitating when he heard a noise downstairs. It had sounded like the front door closing. Frowning, Gabriel waited, listening. Yes, there was definitely someone moving around inside the house. More curious than concerned, he wrapped the towel around his waist and left his bedroom, moving silently down the stairs to investigate the trespass into his new domain. The noises were louder now. He tiptoed in the direction from which they came, pausing in the shadows of the unlit passageway to look through the door into a large, homely farmhouse kitchen.

A brindle-and-white greyhound lay on the stone-flagged floor, its head on its paws, solemnly watching the movements of the woman who was moving about as if she owned the place. Guessing her age to be in the late twenties, Gabriel's gaze lingered on her with as much intensity as the dog's, warmth and pure masculine appreciation spearing through him, catching him by surprise.

A bunch of home-cut flowers, dahlias and chrysanthemums amongst them, were arranged haphazardly in an old stoneware jug on the table, while several carrier bags littered the polished wooden work surfaces. Humming an unrecognisable tune, the woman busied herself stocking the kitchen cupboards with her purchases, her movements athletically graceful. Tight white jeans accentuated the length of her legs and lovingly moulded the rounded swell of her derrière. As she turned round, still unaware of his presence, he could see how the super-soft angora jumper she wore skimmed her shapely frame, outlining the curves of full, firm breasts. The lavender colour set off the natural paler highlights in her light brown hair and lent an amethyst glow to what he could see, even from this distance, were gorgeous grey eyes. Gabriel was mesmerised. Who was this woman?

Picking up a carton of milk and a box of eggs, she twirled her way to the fridge on trainer-clad feet, presenting him with a delectable view of her feminine curves as she bent over, her hips swaying provocatively to the music she heard in her head. Left loose, her wavy hair cascaded round her shoulders in a darkly golden curtain. She flicked it back with one hand as she rose and returned to the counter, still humming to herself as she delved into the carrier bags once more.

Intrigued, Gabriel stepped into the room. The dog was the first to acknowledge him. Anxious brown eyes turned his way, then the too-thin creature whined and all but crawled towards the woman, who leaned down to stroke it with gentle care.

'What's wrong, Foxy?'

Knowing whatever he did was going to startle her, Gabriel cleared his throat, announcing his presence as he walked forward. 'Hello.'

With a shocked cry, the woman swung round, the pack of pasta shells in her hands dropping to the floor. Beautiful smoky grey eyes widened between long, dark lashes as she stared at him, and lushly kissable lips parted in surprise. Her tongue-tip peeped out to moisten them as she stepped back a pace, one hand dropping to calm the fretful dog pressed against her legs, the other curled to a fist at her throat. Gabriel felt her gaze skim over his scantily clad frame and an unexpected but immediate wave of attraction crashed through him.

'I'm sorry.' He offered a smile with the apology, unable to look away from her. 'I didn't mean to scare you. I heard a noise down here and had no idea anyone was around.'

'OK. Um…hello,' she greeted after a moment, her voice melodious but with a husky undertone that appealed to him. Hell, everything about her appealed to him. 'You must be Dr Devereux. I wasn't expecting you until tomorrow,' she continued, bending to pick up the fallen pasta, fumbling briefly as she set it awkwardly back on the counter. With a sudden smile that had the same effect on him as a punch to the solar plexus, she held out her hand. 'I'm Lauren Nightingale…your neighbour at Gatehouse Cottage and also physiotherapist at the Penhally Bay Surgery.'

This was the woman Nick Tremayne had spoken of? *Ooh la la!* 'Lauren, it is a pleasure to meet you. Please, call me Gabriel,' he invited, trying to pull himself together and remember his manners.

Closing the remaining gap between them, he took her graceful hand in his. Her grip was strong, her fingers slender but capable. Looking down, he noted how much paler her warm, satiny skin was than his, how her bones were far more delicate. A jolt of electricity zinged up his arm and along his nerve endings at the contact between them. That Lauren felt it, too, was apparent by the way she bit her lip, her pupils dilating, her body momentarily swaying towards him before she caught herself and pulled back, withdrawing her hand. Gabriel released her with reluctance.

Close to, she was taller than he had realised, five-seven or -eight, he judged, and even more attractive than he had first thought. She had an earthy allure quite unlike the sophisticated, deliberate beauty of some of the Parisian women he had dated in the past but vastly more entrancing and natural. A subtle, floral scent—sweet peas, he recognised—mingled with her unique femininity, teasing and enticing him. No make-up was needed to enhance her flawless skin. Pale gold from a fading summer tan, it looked as smooth as silk. His fingers longed to touch, to discover if she was as warm and soft all over as her hand had felt in his. He struggled to rein back the runaway thoughts but it wasn't easy when every particle of his being hummed with awareness while she studied him as closely as he had regarded her.

Dr Gabriel Devereux was the most delicious surprise!

Fearing that her legs would not hold her upright much

longer, Lauren leaned against the kitchen counter and affected what she hoped was a nonchalant pose. She didn't *feel* remotely nonchalant. Any minute now she was going to do something uncharacteristically shocking, impulsive and embarrassing…like throw herself wantonly into his arms and ravish him.

Gabriel's sudden arrival had taken her off guard. She was disconcerted that she had not been aware of his presence and wondered how long he had stood there watching her. But the fact that she had not seen him in the shadows and had only formed a distinct visual impression when he had stepped into the brightly lit kitchen stirred inner anxieties she was unwilling to deal with. That he was wearing only an ivory towel was a suitable diversion, however, and she grabbed the excuse to ignore her disturbing concerns, unable to resist the temptation to observe him in detail.

She saw bare bodies, or bits of bodies, every working day, but she had never seen one that made her heart hammer, her mouth water and that robbed her of breath as Gabriel's did. Goodness! Her hands clung to the counter as she greedily inspected him. She feared she was about to melt into a puddle at his feet. Nice feet, too, she couldn't help but notice. Very nice. Like the rest of him. Her gaze slowly climbed back up his scrumptious frame.

Strong, lean legs were braced hip-width apart and the towel slung low around his hips revealed a tantalising glimpse of pleasingly muscled, hair-brushed thighs. A narrow line of dark hair in the centre of his flat stomach dipped past his navel and disappeared below the towel. She licked her lips, resisting the urge to touch as she looked over his perfect athletic body, toned abdomen, well-defined chest and broad shoulders, all supple flesh and rippling muscle. He'd clearly just stepped out of the shower as droplets of water glistened on his delicious dark caramel skin, its colour hinting at a French

Caribbean ancestry. Lauren swallowed, battling against the overwhelming desire to press her lips to that warm, damp masculine flesh. She still remembered the faint scent of him when they had been close and shaken hands…tangy citrus soap and clean male, heady and earthy and arousing.

Topping six feet, he was more than impressive. The close-cropped dark hair suited him, accentuating the classically beautiful but supremely masculine bone structure of his face, the slash of high cheekbones, the straight nose and the carved lines of his jaw. Her palm itched to smooth over his head, to feel if the razor-short hair was rough or soft to the touch. His mouth was undeniably sexy, his bronze lips sensually curved and designed for kissing. She yearned to press her own against them, to learn the shape and feel and taste of him.

Twin dimples creased his cheeks when he smiled, while laughter lines fanned out from the corners of his eyes, adding character and hinting at an active sense of humour. Finally, she looked into those thickly lashed eyes. They were the richest brown she had ever seen. As Gabriel met and held her gaze, his pupils dilated, darkening the irises to the colour of finest coffee. The flare of masculine interest was unmistakable and caused a tightening ache of want in the pit of her stomach that was so strong and so sudden she barely suppressed a gasp.

What in the world had come over her? Yes, it had been a while since she had enjoyed male companionship. She had broken up with her long-term boyfriend, Martin Bennett, six months ago, but to all intents and purposes they had been apart a long time before that. They had gone their separate ways amicably, both knowing their lingering on-again-off-again relationship had been based more on old friendship than grand passion and had been leading nowhere. Martin was desperate to get out of Cornwall, to explore and experience new things, while Lauren was content to remain in Penhally, enjoying her job, her friends and her hobbies, including her painting.

Unwelcome and worrying thoughts intruded once more. She hadn't painted much lately and she wasn't anywhere near ready to face the reasons why. Determinedly, she returned her full attention to the exquisite man before her, a quiver running through her at his thorough inspection, as if he had touched her physically.

Since midwife Kate Althorp had met Gabriel at Nick's house in the summer, she had reported that Penhally was in for a treat when the French doctor arrived in their midst. Kate's comments had caused some of their colleagues to tease Lauren about her soon-to-be neighbour. Lauren had ignored the ribbing. But now she could acknowledge first hand that Kate had not been exaggerating. Dear heaven, the man was *gorgeous*!

That Gabriel Devereux would be close by, at home and at work, for the next twelve months was wonderfully thrilling. Already the year ahead was filled with new and unexpected possibilities. Everything feminine within her stood to attention and all the hormones that had been switched off and un-interested since long before her split from Martin now started doing a happy dance like over-enthusiastic cheerleaders. She looked into Gabriel's eyes, excited by the answering desire she saw there. Oh, yes! She was most definitely interested! She just hoped he was in England alone, uninvolved, and had no wife or girlfriend tucked away at home in France.

'It is kind of you to bring things for the kitchen, Lauren,' Gabriel said, the dimples forming in his lean cheeks, his eyes crinkling as he smiled.

She could drown in that smile. And as for his accent, the way he said her name… He made her tingle all over. His English was perfect but delivered with a soft burr and all the Gallic charm imaginable. There was so much she wanted to learn about him but she reined in her rush of questions, scared that she would frighten him away before he'd even properly arrived. There would be time in the days and weeks ahead to

explore the inexplicable and immediate connection she felt
with this man. Or so she hoped. Better to play it cool for now.

'It's no trouble,' she answered, not sure how she managed
to form any words at all, let alone sensible ones. 'I promised
Nick I would make sure you had all you needed.'

Relaxed and at ease, he folded his arms across his chest,
the play of muscle distracting her. 'Thank you. I am sorry I
took you by surprise arriving early.'

'No problem.' Returning his smile, she couldn't prevent
herself looking over his superb body once more. Oh, it was
no problem at all!

'Are you also responsible for airing the house and providing the clean linen and towels?'

'Yes.' Almost overcome with nervous anticipation, she
tucked some strands of hair behind one ear, her hand unsteady.
'Is everything all right?'

'Very much so. I was planning to ask the solicitor who to
thank for making the house feel so welcoming.'

'I'm glad to help,' she assured him, warmed through and
pleased by his thoughtfulness.

He watched her for a long moment, then glanced at the
greyhound who whined and nudged against her legs. 'And
who is your companion?'

'This is Foxy. He lost his owner in the flood and was found
distressed after searching the rubble,' she explained, a catch
in her voice as she gently stroked the dog. 'Both the RSPCA
and Lizzie Chamberlain, who runs the local kennels, were
overrun with extra work and animals needing help during the
crisis. Foxy was always nervous of people, but he knew me
and we bonded, so I was happy to give him a home. He's adjusting but still wary. At least he's started eating again. He
needs time and lots of love.'

The approval and flash of admiration in Gabriel's eyes made
her feel good. She held her breath as he turned his attention to

Foxy. Speaking softly, he hunkered down and held out his hand for the dog to sniff. Calm and patient, he waited for the dog to be comfortable, making no sudden moves. Lauren was surprised and delighted when Foxy inched forward and allowed Gabriel to touch him, something he had permitted few people but her to do in the last ten days. Slowly he was forming a tentative bond with her friends Chloe and Oliver. Foxy's current reaction and his instinct to trust Gabriel was more than interesting and told her much about this intriguing man.

As if satisfied with the early progress, Gabriel didn't push things, moving carefully back and rising before returning his attention to her, causing her heart to pound once more.

'Nick mentioned the flood in an email but I had no idea how bad things were. I was shocked when I drove through town.' He paused, a pout of consideration shaping his mouth and giving her all manner of wicked ideas. 'Are you busy this afternoon, Lauren? Do you have plans?'

'No. Why?' She was filled with sudden hope that she might be able to spend more time with Gabriel. She wasn't ready to leave just yet.

'I was going to make myself a late lunch. Will you join me? It would be good to talk, to learn more about Penhally and the surgery…and what has gone on in the last couple of weeks.'

Not wanting to appear as shamefully eager as she felt, she forced herself not to rush her agreement. Maybe Gabriel's reasons for asking her to linger weren't all she had hoped for, but at this point she would accept any opportunity to enjoy his company. Who knew where things might lead?

'OK.' She cursed the breathlessness of her voice but could do nothing to temper her excitement. 'I can stay a while longer.'

At Lauren's confirmation, Gabriel felt a wash of relief course through him and he expelled the breath he had not realised he had been holding. He was nowhere near ready to let her go.

This was ridiculous. He felt like some gauche sixteen-year-old boy with a crush, rather than the thirty-six-year-old man he really was. Then Lauren looked over him once more and his body instantly heated and tightened in response, as if her touch had been an actual caress. He hoped the loose towel hid the evidence of the arousing effect she had on him.

'Give me five minutes to get dressed,' he requested as he turned away and headed to the door.

'Gabriel?'

Her soft voice halted him and he glanced back. 'Yes?'

'I could prepare a quick meal while you're gone,' she offered.

'Are you sure?'

Her head bobbed in assent. 'It's no trouble. Is there anything you don't like?'

Dieu! He couldn't imagine anything Lauren could suggest that he wouldn't like, but he managed to focus his attention on food. 'Mushrooms, shellfish and red meat,' he informed her, catching her surprised smile.

'Me, too.' Mischief gleamed in her eyes. 'And I confess I'm not keen on boiled cabbage, tapioca or mushy peas either.'

'Believe me, Lauren, you are not alone!' Chuckling, he left the room.

'I certainly hope not—not any more.'

Had he really heard those final whispered words? And could they mean what he hoped they did? He was confused by his instinctive response to this woman. It was unlike him. And that was disturbing. He'd not been so spontaneously attracted to anyone for years—if ever. The timing was unfortunate. He had never considered such a thing happening to him, especially not while part of his world was in turmoil and he had decisions to make about his future. Coming here was meant to give him space to declutter his life, not add more complications to it.

But he couldn't deny the way his body had reacted to the

sight, scent and sound of Lauren Nightingale. Anxious to dress and return to the kitchen as quickly as possible, Gabriel hurried up the stairs. Had he dreamed it all? What if the sizzle of electricity between himself and Lauren had been a figment of his overactive imagination? What if it wasn't? He was here for a year. To work. To think. Did he even want to consider any kind of involvement? He hadn't been at the Manor House an hour and already he was feeling alive at an unexpected awareness, filled with a sense of wary excitement at the possibilities that might lie ahead.

Perhaps it had just been too long since he had dated a woman. After his most recent experience with Adèle, and with his mother's continued interference, he had become cautious, untrusting. But that had been a year ago. And Lauren knew nothing about his life—or his family circumstances. More importantly, Yvette, his mother, knew nothing about Lauren. If anything happened between them, it would be because of who and what they were…no ulterior motives, no deception, no scheming.

Unzipping a suitcase, he pulled out fresh clothes and dressed in record time, favouring casual jeans and a warm cashmere jumper. As he made his way out of his bedroom, tantalising aromas teased his senses and sharpened his hunger, and he increased his pace, keen to discover both the food awaiting him and the intriguing woman who was preparing it.

Lauren occupied his thoughts. He would be cautious about rushing into anything, but he wanted to spend time with her, to get to know her better. If the connection and charge of desire he had felt between them *was* real…

CHAPTER TWO

LAUREN set the plate of food she had prepared on the table in the rustic kitchen and tried very hard not to stare at Gabriel. An impossible feat. He looked almost as gorgeous with his clothes *on*…and just as impressive. The sweater he wore—over the kind of faded, body-hugging jeans that ought to be made illegal, so lethal were they to a woman's blood pressure—looked expensive, the mulberry colour warming and flattering the espresso-coffee tones of his skin.

He sat down, a quizzical expression on his face as he noted she had only laid one place. 'You are not eating, Lauren?'

'No.' The breathlessness was back in her voice—an uncharacteristic reaction that seemed to afflict her at every sight and sound of Gabriel Devereux. 'I met up with friends in town. We had soup and sandwiches at the farmers' market.'

'But you will join me here, yes?' He drew out the chair nearest to him before extending a hand and inviting her to sit.

Gratified by his suggestion to be near him, Lauren hastened to take her seat, hoping she looked far less flustered than she felt. 'Thank you.' For goodness' sake. She was a thirty-year-old woman, not some blushing schoolgirl!

'Forgive me tucking right in, I'm hungrier than I thought.' The appreciative look he sent her, and the readiness of his smile, heated her right through. So much for cool, calm maturity. 'This looks and smells wonderful.'

Cooking was not her greatest talent, but Gabriel gave every evidence of liking her food. She'd made him a simple omelette with cheese and chives, serving it with a warmed granary roll, plus a tomato, rocket and watercress salad…all fresh ingredients she had picked up on her shopping trip that morning. He was eating with relish, his enjoyment making her smile with relief. And she had even more to be grateful for, she admitted to herself—she'd not had any accidents or set fire to the kitchen which, given her current run of clumsy *faux pas*, was a major achievement.

Foxy, having quenched his thirst from the bowl of water she had set down for him, now sprawled his long, too-skinny body beside her chair, his paws twitching in his sleep, blissfully unconcerned by the electrically charged atmosphere crackling between the two humans. Lauren couldn't help but be aware of it. Aware of Gabriel. She was glad she had made herself some tea. It gave her something to do with her hands. Anything to avoid the temptation—the compulsion—to touch him. She cupped the mug, watching from beneath her lashes as he finished his meal. When she raised the mug to her lips and took a sip of her drink, she looked up to find mocha eyes watching her intently, and a fresh dart of feminine recognition zinged through her body.

'That was delicious.' Gabriel's smile and sexy accent undid her every time. 'Thank you, Lauren.'

'My pleasure.'

After taking a drink from his glass of water, he turned so he was facing her, giving her his undivided attention. She could feel fresh heat tinge her cheeks. 'It seems a long time since breakfast.'

'Did you come over from France this morning?' she ventured, struggling to appear cool and composed.

'I took the chance of an earlier ferry from Cherbourg to Poole yesterday, then I stayed the night with an old friend in Bournemouth before driving down here today.'

A bleakness shadowed his eyes, so fleeting it was gone before she could be sure. But she was left with a sense that there was more to Gabriel's departure from France than he had let on. She wondered what had happened, and whether there was a woman involved.

Instead of satisfying her curiosity and asking outright, she endeavoured to be more subtle. 'Wouldn't getting a ferry to Plymouth have been easier?'

'Not really. Cherbourg is only about thirty or forty minutes from where I was based in St Ouen-sur-Mer. If I had gone to Plymouth, it would have meant a long drive through France to Roscoff and almost twice as long for the Channel crossing.' His eyes twinkled as he sent her a wry smile. 'I am not the best traveller on ferries! And I prefer to be in control of my own destiny. Besides, the drive down from Dorset to Cornwall today gave me the opportunity to reaccustom myself to English roads.'

'How did you come to take this job?' she asked, propping her chin in one hand as she looked at him.

'I volunteered.' Pushing his empty plate aside, he leaned closer and rested one forearm on the table. 'I was only working in St Ouen-sur-Mer on a temporary basis to help out a friend from medical school. François is head of the clinic and his wife, Celeste, is also a doctor there. Another of the partners, Marianne, had a baby last Christmas and was on maternity leave. Then, in early January, François badly broke his leg in a skiing accident. He was having trouble finding a replacement doctor, so he called me. As I had reason to leave Paris for a while, I was happy to provide cover. I've been there ever since. But now François is back on his feet and Marianne is ready to return to work. It was time for me to move on.'

'I see,' Lauren murmured, toying with the handle of her mug. Clearly Gabriel was loyal to his friends and ready to help in a crisis, but she wondered what had made him so eager to leave Paris in a hurry at the start of the year. He had sounded relieved to have received François's initial call…and now to be in Cornwall.

'When the position came up to work here for a year, I was interested in taking it,' he continued, and she lost herself in the sound of his huskily accented voice, captivated by the way he looked at her, maintaining eye contact as though she was interesting and important to him. 'I speak English—'

'Perfect English,' she interjected, halting his explanation.

An amused smile curved his mouth at her praise. 'Thank you, *chérie*.'

'Sorry, I interrupted you.' She smothered a groan of embarrassment.

'That's all right.' Her skin tingled as Gabriel briefly reached out and whispered his fingertips across the back of her hand. She sucked in a shaky breath and struggled to concentrate as he continued to speak about his reasons for moving to Penhally. 'I was the only doctor at the clinic who was single and without commitments…the others did not want to uproot their families to come here. And I've worked in England before—in London. I enjoyed it, but I was eager to experience small-town, rural medicine, too.'

Again Lauren thought there was more to the story than he had told her, but she was exceedingly glad he was here. She had also noted with a shiver of hopeful anticipation his comment that he was single and had no commitments. Surely that was a good sign? She had no idea why, but she had felt a deep connection with and recognition of this man from the outset.

'So, Lauren, tell me about the flood.' Gabriel broke the silence, drawing her from her thoughts. 'What happened?

How much damage has there been? You said Foxy's owner
was tragically killed but was anyone else hurt?'

Lauren huffed out a breath, taking a few moments as she
wondered where to begin recounting the events of that never-
to-be-forgotten and emotional day.

As Gabriel waited for Lauren to speak, he resisted the fierce
urge to keep touching her, remembering how silky her skin
had felt beneath his fingers. Instead, he reflected on what he
had told her about himself and his reasons for coming to
Cornwall, hoping he had said enough to curb her interest
without giving away any of his secrets…or his inner turmoil.

It was true that the request from François in January to help
out in his clinic on Normandy's west coast could not have
come at a better time. He had been deeply sorry for the injury
that had caused François so many problems, but his friend's
need had provided Gabriel with the chance to leave Paris—
and Yvette—far behind. Time away to come to terms with all
he had suddenly learned about his family, and to put space
between himself and home, had been exactly what he had
needed. But that space had not proved great enough, so the
offer to work in Penhally Bay had been even more welcome.
The width of the English Channel would surely be a suitable
barrier. Here in Cornwall he felt he could breathe again and
hear himself think.

His early departure from France had been sparked by
another summons from home—one more demand, one more
threat he had chosen to ignore. Things were increasingly
strained with his mother. Not that Yvette Devereux had ever
been particularly *motherly* towards him, he reflected with a
cynical twist of his lips. She had never been the warm, nur-
turing and understanding type, but always stiff, distant, with
her rigid view of duty and propriety. Now he knew why.

A light touch on his arm startled him from his disturbing

thoughts and he glanced up to find Lauren watching him with a frown on her face.

'Are you all right, Gabriel?'

'Yes, of course.' His skin felt warm and alive long after her fingers had been withdrawn. He managed a smile, grateful for the interruption and thankful to push family troubles to the back of his mind again. 'I was miles away. Please, you were going to explain the events of the last couple of weeks.'

'You hear about these things happening, but you never expect them to affect your own community,' she began, a serious tone to her voice. 'We had no warning. The sky went black, there was thunder and lightning, and the most torrential rain I've ever seen or heard. It poured off everything. Combined with the run-off inland, something collapsed upstream and the deluge swelled watercourses, causing a flash flood that swept away everything in its path. The river Lanson burst its banks, funnelling massive amounts of earthy-black water laden with debris down through the centre of Penhally, hitting us full force.'

'What happened to you?' Gabriel asked with concern, noting how Lauren shivered, rubbing her forearms in reaction. 'Were you caught out in it?'

'I was lucky. I was visiting a patient at the time. The power went out, the telephone lines were down and mobile phone coverage was patchy, but I received a message to go to one of the two evacuation points. I spent the rest of the time at the school, helping out.' She raised her gaze to his, her eyes registering grief. 'It was really frightening. People were missing, we didn't know what had happened to friends. There were a number of minor injuries, some more serious ones…and two people died.'

Gabriel listened to Lauren's explanation of the disaster with shock. '*Dieu*. I had no idea things were so bad,' he murmured, taking one of her trembling hands in his, needing to comfort, to touch her. 'I am so sorry. It must have been horribly traumatic and such a loss for the whole community.'

'Yes, it was. Is.' Hearing the waver in her voice, he tightened his hold on her hand, linking their fingers and brushing the pad of his thumb across her wrist. 'Audrey Baxter was one of our regular patients at the surgery. Elderly and with health problems, she was a bit of a busybody but she meant well. She had recently taken Foxy in as a companion from the rescue centre and having him helped her emotional well-being considerably. They helped each other, I suppose. Anyway, Audrey was caught outside when the flash flood came. She never stood a chance with that wall of water. The local vicar, Reverend Kenner, plunged in to try to save her, but he was lost, too, when the end of the Anchor Hotel collapsed on them. He was such a good man. He did a great deal for this community. And it was tragic for his daughter, Rachel. She's just a teenager, and with her mother dying a few years ago her father was all she had. They were very close. Now she's pregnant and alone. Her aunt and uncle in Plymouth are caring for her.'

'Lauren,' he murmured, wishing he had the words to ease the pain and horror of what she and the rest of the town had been through.

'It's all so unfair!'

'I know.' He stroked her arm, aware of the softness of her skin and the beat of her pulse. 'Sometimes it is impossible to understand why these things happen.'

Her fingers returned the pressure of his and she looked at him with a sorrowful smile. 'That's the truth.' She shook her head, a sigh escaping.

'Thank goodness you had such excellent rescue aid or things could have been even worse for the town.'

'Yes, we were very grateful. I think people are finding it hard to accept we've been affected like this again. It's not that long since Penhally's last great tragedy. The big storm ten years ago took many lives, including those of Kate Althorp's husband James and Nick Tremayne's father and brother.'

'How are people coping now?' Gabriel asked after a short silence, one that saw them both lost in thought.

'A lot are still displaced after the flood. The caravan park above the cliffs on Mevagissey Road has taken in several families, while others are staying with relatives and friends or renting temporary accommodation.'

'It looked as though much has been done to begin clearing up.'

Lauren nodded, her voice stronger again now. 'Everyone has worked very hard. It's amazing the mess and damage water can cause. I think it will be months before some of the homes are fit to be lived in again.'

'Many of your patients must be needing extra care and understanding,' Gabriel allowed, looking down at their joined hands, thankful that Lauren had not pulled away.

'Yes, there's been trauma and anxiety. And it's hard for some to come to terms with losing irreplaceable and sentimental possessions. We also had to be careful because of things like polluted water and so on as some people failed to heed the safety advice in the aftermath.'

Gabriel watched as she tucked a couple of wayward strands of hair behind her ear. Adjusting his hold on her hand, he played with her fingers and traced a circle on her palm with his thumb, aware of the growing connection between them.

'So, tell me about your regular patients,' he suggested after a few moments, relieved to see a lightening of her expression.

He listened with interest as Lauren talked of little Timmy Morrison, nearly five months old and diagnosed at birth with cystic fibrosis, of eleven-year-old Paul Mitchell, coping spiritedly with Duchenne muscular dystrophy, and of older patients like Harry Biscombe in sheltered accommodation at

Gow Court, with osteoporosis, whom she had been visiting when the flood had hit, and Stella Chamberlain, currently in the Harbour View Nursing Home with Parkinson's disease.

'Stella's desperate to go home but it's becoming impossible for her daughter Lizzie to cope. It's very sad. We're all doing the best we can to find the best solution for both Stella and Lizzie.'

Every word Lauren spoke, both about the regulars she visited at home and her more mobile and short-term patients who came to the surgery, revealed how dedicated she was and just how much she cared about each and every person. Minute by minute Gabriel was more impressed with Lauren Nightingale. Her natural beauty had first appealed to him and he had been unable to ignore the sparks of attraction that had crackled between them from the first moment. He had only just met her and yet the more he knew about her, the longer they talked, the more he respected and admired her as a person. She was funny, intelligent and caring. Genuine, without any airs or graces.

Meeting Lauren put an interesting and unexpected slant on his time in Cornwall. Her eyes reflected a feminine interest she made no effort to hide and he felt the answering response rise within him, one he had not felt in a long time. This might well turn out to be an even more interesting year than he had ever imagined.

'I'm not sure which patients you'll be seeing,' Lauren told him now, explaining about the staffing at the surgery and how GP Dragan Lovak was taking time off to be with his wife after the recent birth of their baby boy. 'I expect Nick will suggest you spend time with one of the other doctors this week—if you are lucky, it will be Oliver Fawkner.' The affection in her voice as she mentioned the other doctor brought a flash of unexpected jealousy. 'If Nick agrees, it would also be good if you could come out on house calls with various members of staff.'

'Including you?'

'Probably.'

His gaze caught hers. 'I hope so.'

'Me, too.' She bit her lip, her eyes widening as she realised she had spoken aloud. He felt the kick of her pulse beneath his fingers as she hurried on. 'There have been some changes due to the surgery expansion—you'll see those when you look around on Monday. Immediately after the flood, Nick asked us all not to go out on calls after dark unless it was an emergency, because of all the debris and possible danger of unsafe buildings and falling masonry.' Gabriel nodded, knowing it made sense not to put more people at risk than necessary. 'That ban has been lifted since the clean-up started,' Lauren continued. 'But I've kept to the new schedule. It works for me and my patients now we have the new physiotherapy room. With Nick's agreement, I do house calls that are required in the mornings and see patients at the surgery in the afternoons.'

'So I'll keep at least one morning free to go on visits with you.'

Gabriel's statement brought fresh warmth to her cheeks. 'OK,' she agreed, already eager for the time they would spend together, even if it was work related. That he was so keen and interested in her patients and the work she did brought her a glow of pleasure.

He asked more questions about the surgery, staff and the town in general, and she was happy to answer them, to help him fit into his new role in a different country. They had clicked from the first and got on so well she felt she had known him for ever. Yet all the time there was the undercurrent of sexual tension, the hum of desire between them, and excitement bubbled inside her at what might happen.

She had not forgotten for a moment that her hand was still in his, their fingers entwined, but she had no desire to let go until he did. They talked about local activities and their hobbies, discovering shared interests in books and music. They both loved sport, but while Lauren was keen on running, swimming and cycling, Gabriel favoured team sports like football. She could listen to him for ever with that sexy accent and soft huskiness edging his voice.

'So you jog every morning?' he asked now, pulling her from her thoughts.

'Yes, I try to do between three and five miles a day.'

'I can see it keeps you fit.'

The knot in her stomach tightened as he looked her over, the expression in his melting brown eyes letting her know that he liked what he saw. 'I try.' She swallowed the restriction in her throat, a tingle running through her as his thumb began to brush across her palm and wrist once more. 'I've done a few triathlons in the past but I don't get the chance to compete much these days.'

'Do you prefer to run alone, or do you enjoy company?'

'Company is good,' she murmured, hoping that meant he might join her one day. 'If you still play football, you should talk to Oliver. He's organising a charity match next weekend to raise money for the flood relief fund.'

'That's an excellent idea, I'll do that. Lauren—'

Whatever Gabriel had been about to say was halted by the sudden beep of her mobile phone announcing an incoming text message. Lauren jumped at the intrusion, disappointed when her hand was released. Already she missed the contact between them. Beside her, Foxy stirred at the noise, stretching and yawning before rising to his feet and nudging her leg. Absently, she stroked his head with one hand while rummaging in her bag with the other to find her phone.

'Sorry about this.'

'Don't worry,' Gabriel reassured her, but he looked as regretful for the interruption as she was.

Sighing, Lauren tilted the phone, frowning as she concentrated on reading the message, aware it was harder to see the small letters illuminated on the screen than it had once been. Again, she pushed the concern away, unable to face the implications. The text, she discovered, was from her friend Chloe MacKinnon.

'Worried you aren't home yet. Any problems? Oliver says supper ready in an hour. Love C x'

Shocked, Lauren looked towards the windows and saw how dark it was outside. She glanced at her watch, stunned to discover the time. 'Oh, my gosh!'

'Everything all right?' Gabriel asked.

'I'd no idea it was this late. I'm so sorry, I've taken up all your afternoon!'

Laughing, his hand brushed her arm. 'I've enjoyed every moment with you, Lauren. Thank you. I am the one who should apologise for detaining you.'

'It's fine. I just didn't say I was delayed. I was expected home ages ago.'

'I see.' Gabriel moved back from her, disappointment dulling his eyes.

Her breath caught as she realised what he thought. 'I've told you about my friends Chloe and Oliver, midwife and GP at the surgery?' she asked, and he nodded. 'They're engaged and Oliver's been living at Chloe's cottage in Fisherman's Row since the end of July. They were flooded out and have been staying with me since then,' she rushed to explain, gratified to see relief lighten his expression.

'So there's no boyfriend waiting for you?'

'No. There's no one.' She responded to his blunt question with equal clarity. 'But I'd better get back.'

'Of course.'

Reluctantly, she rose to her feet, unhooked her bag from the back of the chair and looped the strap over her shoulder. 'Is there anything else I can do? Do you have all you need?'

She looked around the kitchen, hoping she had remembered everything.

'It's fine, Lauren. You have done so much and I appreciate it.'

'If you think of anything…'

'I'll let you know,' he promised with a smile.

'I wrote out some phone numbers for you.' Including her own, she added silently, pointing to the fridge where a piece of paper was held firm by a colourful Penhally magnet. With nothing else to prevent her leaving, she slipped on Foxy's lead and turned towards the door. 'I'd better go, then.'

She was acutely conscious of Gabriel following close behind her as she walked out of the kitchen. Pausing a moment, she formed a picture in her mind of the dim, unlit hallway and the route to the front door, trying to remember if there was anything in the way. She didn't think so…provided she avoided the bottom tread of the stairs that stuck out a few inches on her left. Anxiety gripped her as she was faced with her failing night vision. She could fumble for an unseen light switch and risk drawing attention to her problem, or take a chance the hall was clear. She chose the latter.

A short while ago she had breezily told Gabriel about her altered working hours. What she had not told him was how she had used the cover of the flood disaster and completion of the new physio room to make her changed schedule permanent. A flicker of guilt assailed her for the deception and for hiding her real reasons from Nick and everyone else. She was afraid to venture out after dark and, with each passing autumn day, dusk was falling earlier. The only journey she felt able to make at night was from the surgery to her cottage, a route she knew so well she could cover every inch of the short distance with her eyes closed. Which was how it had felt lately in the dark. She was scared what it meant, but was unable to face the fact that something strange was happening to her sight. At some point, if it got worse, she would have to. She would never put other people in danger. But for now she could still cover it up.

After she had negotiated the hallway slowly but safely, Gabriel reached round her to open the door, momentarily bringing their bodies into close proximity and firing her blood once more. Before he could put on the outside light, she moved forward, missing her step, unable to see. For a second, she teetered off balance, then Gabriel's arm was there to steady her. The light came on and she blinked, disoriented for a second, aware, when her vision sharpened, of the frown on his face.

'Are you OK?'

'Yes, fine,' she assured him breathlessly. With caution, she stepped out of his hold and down the steps to the gravel drive. Needing to disguise her latest mishap, she turned back to smile at him. 'There is something you should know about me before you hear it from anyone else.'

The wariness returned to his eyes and she could sense his tension. 'What's that?'

'I'm renowned for being impossibly clumsy.' She managed a passable laugh, trying not to think of her catalogue of stupid incidents. Unfortunately they seemed to be happening more and more often, her most recent examples being the moment she had inexplicably reversed into a parked car at the church after Jack and Alison's wedding, and the way she had stumbled and fallen in the rubble the day after the flood. 'Everyone teases me for being an accident waiting to happen.'

'I'll consider myself warned,' Gabriel replied, his answering laugh not completely masking his confusion.

Eager to leave on a more positive note, Lauren lingered. 'If you have nothing else planned, would you like to come for lunch tomorrow? You can meet Chloe and Oliver...get to know them before work on Monday.'

'I'd love to.' A teasing glint flickered in his eyes. 'Not the roast beef?'

'No! Chicken and all the trimmings. And Chloe is doing one of her special puddings,' she told him, laughing back.

'What time?'

'About noon?' She tried to sound casual, but already she was brimming with excitement at seeing him again.

'I'll be there,' he promised, making her pulse race. 'Would you like me to walk you back?'

She would, but she didn't want him witnessing her tripping again. 'Thanks, but there's no need.'

'Until tomorrow, then.' His voice dropped to a rough murmur. *'Au revoir, chérie.'*

'Bye.'

She felt him watching her as she walked carefully down the drive, Foxy well behaved at her side. Silently, she counted her steps, having made this journey before. She knew that when she reached the curve, the lights in her cottage would guide her home, but the knowledge that she was seeing less and less at night filled her with silent fear. How long could she hide her secret?

A sigh of relief escaped when her cottage came into view and she picked up her pace, more sure of herself, keen to tell Chloe and Oliver about the exciting new doctor. It was awful that the flood had driven her friends from their home. Chloe had been more upset at her missing cats, but one of the members of the rescue team had found Pirate and Cyclops unscathed on top of a wardrobe upstairs as the waters receded. In the days since they had moved in, Foxy and the cats had negotiated a cautious stand-off.

Until Chloe and Oliver found a suitable new home, Lauren was happy for them to stay with her. She enjoyed their company. But she wondered if things might get a bit awkward should anything develop between herself and Gabriel. There was plenty of time to worry about that, she reassured herself, knowing she shouldn't get too excited even though their first meeting had left her in no doubt about the connection between them. However foolish, she sensed that something unusual and important could evolve in the days and weeks ahead.

'We were going to send out a search party!' Chloe teased when Lauren let herself in, took off Foxy's lead and walked into the living room.

Her friend was cuddled up in Oliver's lap on the sofa in front of a roaring log fire. It didn't take a genius to know from their rumpled clothes and tousled hair what they had been doing with their extra time alone. Lauren was delighted for Chloe but it was ironic that her friend—who had suffered an abusive past at the hands of her brutal father, and who had remained a virgin until Oliver had come into her life—had enjoyed a more varied and extensive sex life in three months than Lauren had in ten years. She didn't begrudge Chloe her happiness and pleasure for a moment, but she wouldn't half mind being as lucky.

An image of a certain scrumptious French doctor filled her mind. Oh, yes! Now, there was a man with va-va-voom, one who would surely know how to make a woman feel special. Unable to stop smiling, Lauren sank into an armchair. Her heart was still pounding.

'Sorry you were concerned. I got held up. Dr Devereux had just arrived when I took the shopping up to the Manor House. I stayed for a chat.'

'Some chat,' Chloe commented with a meaningful grin that had Oliver laughing and Lauren's cheeks warming. 'Come on, tell us what happened.'

Nothing…and yet everything. But Lauren didn't know how to explain that. 'We talked about the surgery, Penhally and the flood. Gabriel's coming here for lunch tomorrow. I told him about your football match, Oliver, and he's keen to play.'

'Great! Thanks, Lauren. Nick has suggested that Gabriel shadow me next week, so it will be good to meet him in advance.'

'But what's he like?' Chloe persisted.

Lauren leaned back and sighed, unable to keep her smile from broadening. 'Absolutely *divine*.'

No way was she going to last out Gabriel's time here without being a *very* bad girl.

Hopefully.

CHAPTER THREE

'THANKS again for coming in early this morning, Gabriel. I think we've covered everything,' Nick Tremayne decided, leading the way back to his consulting room after a tour of the revamped surgery. He returned to his chair and rubbed his hands together. 'Do you have any other questions?'

'Is the expansion work nearly complete?' Gabriel had been impressed with the improvements that had taken place since his previous weekend visit in July.

'It won't be long now. Hopefully no more than a week. My daughter Lucy originally worked on the plans for the changes and devised a way to use the dead space we had here to make more room. We've rearranged the layout, adding extra facilities as well as increasing consulting-room availability upstairs and down,' Nick explained. 'There are a few minor jobs to finish, mostly outside, but we've been very lucky…the builders have worked around us so that patient disruption has been kept to a minimum.'

'The new X-ray and plaster rooms on the ground floor must make life much easier.'

'Indeed,' Nick agreed. 'It means we can handle the less serious breaks and injuries here now, rather than having to send everyone on the half-hour journey to the hospital in St Piran. It benefits the hospital, the patients and ourselves. As does having the new physiotherapy room for Lauren,' he added. 'Our workload is increasing all the time—and not just during the tourist season—so your presence here is even more welcome.'

'Thank you.'

Nick shuffled some papers on his desk. 'I've arranged for you to spend a few days working with Oliver Fawkner. You can take your own consultations, of course—we've assigned you one of the new rooms next to Lauren's—but Oliver will help you learn your way around the district. Is that all right with you?'

'But, yes, I appreciate it. I have already met Oliver, Chloe and Lauren—we had lunch together yesterday.'

'Good, good. I'm sure you'll get on well.' Nick nodded with approval, then handed over a sheet of paper. 'Here is this week's roster. We take turns doing out-of-hours cover so no one is unduly burdened, but we won't expect you to do your own evening and weekend calls until you are settled in. Again, as Oliver is temporarily living so close to the Manor House, you can share duties with him for a week or two before we add you to the list to do calls alone.'

'That sounds fine. Maybe I could also make some visits out with other staff?' Gabriel suggested, following up on the idea Lauren had given him.

Nick glanced up, an eyebrow raised in question. 'What did you have in mind?'

'I would be interested in learning how the various disciplines interact here. And it would give me a chance to meet some of the regular patients. Maybe if I spent a morning with the nurses, and also go out on a few home visits with Chloe and Lauren during my first couple of weeks?'

'An excellent idea,' his new boss agreed. His smile of approval stripped some of the characteristic sternness from his face. 'The more familiarisation you can gain, the better. I'll leave you to arrange the details with the staff concerned. You can sort things out to fit your own schedules. I'll mention it when we all meet and—' The phone buzzed and Nick frowned, momentarily distracted. 'Excuse me,' he murmured. 'Yes? Of course, Hazel. We'll be there directly.'

Gabriel visualised Hazel, the practice manager, whom he had met a short while ago during his wander around with Nick. The older woman had been polite while giving him the once-over but appeared to be reserving her judgement about him. He could understand that. Hopefully he would pass muster with her, and the rest of the staff, in time. He was thinking of all he had been told about his new colleagues when Nick set down the phone and reclaimed his attention.

'Pretty much everyone on duty is here now. Come on up to the staffroom, Gabriel, and I'll introduce you,' he invited, rising to his feet.

Glad that their chat had gone well, and looking forward to starting work, Gabriel followed Nick towards the stairs. Although reserved and serious, the senior partner had been welcoming, their discussion informative. Even so, Gabriel was thankful to have had the chance to meet Oliver and Chloe in more informal and relaxed circumstances at Lauren's cottage the previous day. He had thoroughly enjoyed himself. They had lingered over a delicious lunch and talked long into the afternoon. It had been dark by the time he had walked the short distance back to the Manor House feeling content and more comfortable about his new job.

With dark hair and green eyes, Chloe was kind and gentle, as dedicated to her role as a midwife as Lauren was to hers as a physiotherapist. As for Oliver, dark-eyed and with over-long dark hair, Gabriel had liked him from the first, forming an instant friendship with the handsome, charismatic doctor. Oliver was only three years younger than himself and they had quickly established that they shared many interests in common besides their careers, especially a love of sport. Gabriel did not share Oliver's and Chloe's love of motor-

bikes, however. It hadn't needed Lauren to tell him that Oliver
and Chloe were a couple...that they were madly in love was
obvious to anyone who saw them together.

And then there was Lauren herself.

She had been a complete surprise to him and he had not
been able to stop thinking about her since finding her in his
kitchen on Saturday afternoon. He'd been intrigued to learn
she was an accomplished artist. There hadn't been an opportunity to look around her studio the day before but he had seen
a couple of her landscapes hanging in the surgery's reception
area during his tour with Nick. He had found himself drawn
to the paintings even before he had realised they were
Lauren's. She had real talent. He was looking forward to
working with her—and to getting to know her better socially.
Only his early meeting with Nick had prevented him from
joining Lauren for her morning jog. There would be time for
that in the days ahead. And, he hoped, for much more. He still
intended to be cautious, but any resolve to remain uninvolved
had wavered on Saturday and melted entirely on Sunday.

The sound of chatter coming from the staffroom became
louder and drew him from his thoughts. As Nick led the way
inside and an anticipatory silence descended, Gabriel's nervousness at the prospect of meeting his colleagues returned.
He'd never experienced this self-doubt about acceptance until
recently—until his world had turned upside down after his
father's death and things he had thought he had known about
his life, his family, his very identity—had proved to be a lie.
Gabriel swallowed the rush of emotions, forcing his private
issues to the back of his mind. It was good to know there
would be at least a couple of familiar faces here. A quick
glance around the room told him that Lauren had yet to arrive
and he struggled to mask his disappointment. However, Oliver
and Chloe were there, their smiles reassuring him.

Uncomfortable at being the centre of attention, he hoped

his own smile was natural and that he came across as being more relaxed than he felt under the scrutiny he was being subjected to. Thankfully the atmosphere was welcoming, although he imagined some people had similar reservations to those Hazel had exhibited earlier. He remained silent as Nick made the introductions and turned to draw him forward.

'Come on in and join us. Everyone, this is Gabriel Devereux.' His manner benevolent and paternal, Nick gestured around the room. 'You already know Oliver and Chloe. And you remember Kate Althorp, our other midwife, from your visit in the summer?'

'But of course. It's good to see you again, Kate.' As the older woman rose to greet him, he gave her a Gallic kiss on both cheeks. 'How is your son Jem?'

Kate's smile revealed her pleasure. 'He's well. Thank you, Gabriel. Welcome back to Penhally Bay! We are so pleased to have you with us.'

'I am excited to be here.' He smiled back, grateful for Kate's warm approach.

Nick made the other introductions and Gabriel shook hands with the rest of the team. When the formalities were over, Gabriel sat on an empty chair opposite Oliver and Chloe, and accepted the mug Eve Dwyer, one of the practice nurses, handed him.

'We usually start the day with a coffee and a chat,' she explained, her manner friendly. 'Milk and sugar?'

'Just a dash of milk, please.'

As Eve added the milk to his mug and then turned to replace the carton in the fridge, a crash sounded out on the stairway, followed by a string of muffled curses. Gabriel looked round in time to see Nick shaking his head and moving towards the door.

'That must be Lauren.'

Everyone laughed in response to Nick's wry comment, but

the amusement was affectionate, Gabriel realised with some relief, already feeling protective of Lauren. Then he noted the concern on Oliver's face, along with the way Chloe's smile dimmed when she exchanged a glance with her fiancé. Gabriel shared a look with Oliver and as a silent acknowledgement passed between them he felt a shiver of unease. He had known Lauren less than forty-eight hours, but it appeared he was not alone in his impression that something more might lie behind her clumsiness. Gabriel filed the moment away. He would keep his own counsel for now, but Oliver could be the man to talk to if his initial worrying suspicions came to anything.

Looking adorably flustered, and dressed in a uniform of navy blue tunic and trousers, her hair tied back in a ponytail, Lauren hurried into the room. She was carrying a haphazard stack of files and balancing a round tin precariously on top.

'Sorry I'm late. I was delayed downstairs talking with a patient on the phone,' she explained, sounding a touch breathless. 'The waiting room is starting to fill up early—the usual collection of post-weekend crises, no doubt. Hazel is holding the fort and says to carry on without her.'

'Are those some of Hazel's biscuits?' someone asked.

Gabriel watched as Lauren awkwardly juggled the files and manoeuvred the tin so she could prise open the lid. 'Her Cornish fairings,' she announced once she had peeped inside. A twinkle of mischief in her smoky grey eyes, she offered him the tin. 'All Hazel's home-made food treats are favourites here, Gabriel, so I advise you to take what you can before the rest of this unruly lot devour them.'

'Thank you.' It was a bit early in the day for him, but Gabriel accepted one of the biscuits to please Lauren. He tried it with his coffee, surprised how much he enjoyed the ginger-flavoured local delicacy. 'They're excellent.'

'Tell Hazel that and you'll be in her good books for life.' Kate laughed.

'Come on, Lauren, don't hog the tin. I missed breakfast and I'm starving,' GP Adam Donnelly called, growling in mock complaint as others grabbed their share of the biscuits before the tin reached him.

Gabriel was gratified when Lauren chose the chair next to him, her smile and the look in her eyes setting off the zing of awareness he felt every time he saw her.

'A word of warning, Gabriel,' one of the district nurses joked. 'Make sure you park your car well away from Lauren's—if you want to find it in one piece when you go back to it!'

As the tale of her reversing into a car at a recent wedding was recounted, Lauren smiled, taking the ribbing in good part, but Gabriel could see the flash of hurt and worry in her eyes. The belief that there was something more than Lauren just being clumsy nagged at him but he hadn't yet put his finger on what it was that disturbed him. Frowning, he remembered her uneasiness leaving the Manor House on Saturday night and the way she had tripped in the dark. She had explained away her stumble by telling him how accident prone she was, but he had sensed she was covering up for something else. More than once in their short acquaintance he had noticed the way she squinted at her mobile phone screen, tilting it around before reading the message. Then there were the moments she displayed an apparent lack of spatial awareness and misjudgement of distances.

As Nick reclaimed the attention of those in the room, the teasing ceased and Gabriel had to set his considerations about Lauren aside. Instead, he listened with interest as the discussion turned to items of surgery business and any noteworthy out-of-hours incidents with patients. Adam had been called out the previous day to a thirteen-year-old girl with appendicitis who had been admitted to St Piran Hospital, while Kate had attended a mum-to-be who had reported some abdominal pain.

'I'm convinced it is nothing serious but, given her level of anxiety, I've arranged for her to see the consultant at the hospital today instead of next week.'

'Better to be safe than sorry,' Nick remarked, to murmurs of agreement.

Gabriel watched the interaction between Nick and Kate with interest. The tension between the two had been glaringly apparent during the barbecue at Nick's house back in July. He had no idea of their history but he thought it went beyond the doctor-midwife dynamic. Thankfully, the atmosphere between them today was less fraught.

'Gabriel is going to be shadowing Oliver this week, especially on home visits and out-of-hours work,' Nick outlined as the patient reviews came to an end. 'I've also supported his request to spend some time with other staff and will leave you to organise convenient days between you…Lauren, Chloe and the district nurses in particular. Gabriel, enjoy your time here and speak up if you have any queries. I am sure everyone will do all they can to make you welcome and help you settle in for this year-long stay with us.'

Smiling his thanks, Gabriel's attention lingered on Lauren beside him. She had done more than anyone to make him feel comfortable, both at home and work, and her insights and advice had been invaluable. As everyone rose to their feet and began to file out, heading off to attend to their respective duties, Oliver hung back with Chloe.

'We can do a joint list this morning, Gabriel. And when we come back from the house calls, we'll get you set up in your own room. You can take your own surgery slots from this afternoon if you'd care to,' his new friend suggested.

'That suits me.'

'Great.' Oliver smiled and ushered Chloe ahead of him. 'I'll see you downstairs in a few minutes, then.'

Left alone in the staffroom, Gabriel felt Lauren's hand slide into his. Palm to palm. A perfect fit. Delicate yet strong.

And her skin was satin soft. Not at all sorry to be touching her but surprised by her actions, he looked into warm grey eyes.

'Lauren?'

'I just wanted to wish you an enjoyable first day.' Her fingers squeezed his before letting go. He felt the loss of their contact. Then she caught him unawares again, leaning in to press a gentle but all-too-fleeting kiss on his cheek. 'Good luck, Gabriel.'

His skin prickled from the brush of her mouth. Unable to let her go, he caught her hand as she drew away. Her thoughtfulness and caring touched him on an emotional level, while inflaming the physical desire he had felt from the first moment they had met. His body tightened with need for her. He wanted to haul her into his arms and kiss her senseless. Unfortunately he didn't think Nick would be impressed to find the new doctor passionately making out with the physiotherapist in the staffroom on his first day at work!

'Thank you, *chérie*.' He cupped her face with his free hand, relishing the feel of her and the instinctive way she pressed her cheek to his palm. He grazed his thumb across her parted lips, the pad briefly catching on the fullness of the lower one. Her breath hitched, and he watched as her eyes darkened, the desire in them unmistakable. 'I'll see you later.'

'Yes. OK,' she agreed, the husky edge returning to her voice.

He regretted letting her go but he had to. If he kissed her now he wouldn't want to stop. Oliver and their patients were waiting for him downstairs. It was time for him to start work. Time to concentrate on the first day of his new job and think about something other than Lauren…before he lost his head entirely.

Come Friday, Lauren was convinced her lips were still tingling. She licked them, sure she could taste a hint of the masculine tang of Gabriel's skin even now. He'd felt so good. And had smelt delicious, too…earthy and citrusy and all male. She had never been so drawn to and aware of a man before.

The attraction was fierce. Immediate. Scary but incredibly exciting in its intensity.

On Monday morning, dressed in a dark suit, crisp white shirt and ocean-blue tie, Gabriel had looked as if he had just stepped off the catwalk—a star model for the finest Parisian fashion house. She hadn't thought he could look any better than he did in his figure-hugging jeans—or that ivory towel—but suited up for work he'd taken her breath away all over again. He had an aristocratic bearing, one that hinted that he had origins in wealth and status, yet he was completely natural, down-to-earth and unpretentious.

Gabriel's reaction to her good-luck gesture had taken her by surprise. She could still feel the warmth of his palm cupping her face, the stroke of his thumb across her lips, the desire that had flared in his eyes as he had looked deep into her own. She desperately wanted to know what it would be like to kiss him. It was all she had thought about for days. How would it feel? How would he taste? She wanted to touch him. Wanted to feel his hands on her body.

It had been such a hectic week that she hadn't seen Gabriel anywhere near as much as she had hoped to. Not alone, anyway. He had joined her for her morning jog before work on a couple of occasions and he'd come to Gatehouse Cottage for an evening meal some nights. But Oliver and Chloe had been there, too, and there had been far too much talk about work for Lauren's liking. Tomorrow, Saturday, marked the first-week anniversary of when she had met him. Gabriel had morning surgery and then was on call with Oliver for the rest of the day, so there was not going to be much chance for her to see him then. And Sunday was the day of the charity football match. Yet another missed opportunity for some time alone with him. She knew she was behaving like a foolish, thwarted schoolgirl, but she couldn't seem to help herself.

'Are you all right, Lauren?'

Embarrassment made her cheeks turn pink as Mike Trevellyan's voice jolted her from her thoughts. 'I'm so sorry, Mike, I was…distracted.' Guilt surged through her because she had been daydreaming about Gabriel instead of focusing on her patient.

'So I gathered.' Amusement shone in his eyes. 'Anything to do with the new French doctor I've been hearing about?'

'Why would you think that?' Goodness, had the rumour mill started already?

'Kate has mentioned Dr Devereux to Fran several times since meeting him in the summer. She said Penhally was in for a treat when he finally arrived here to work,' Mike explained, his tone teasing. 'And there's been some envy that you are his nearest neighbour. The whisper has gone around that he's impressed many people during his first week here.'

'Gabriel is an excellent doctor,' she allowed, trying to keep her comments professional and hide the pride she was experiencing at the news.

'I'm not sure his medical skills are what interests most of the ladies!'

A wave of possessiveness surged through her. She was unaccustomed to jealousy, but she felt territorial and protective of Gabriel, and she didn't want to think of other women lusting after him. Refusing to react to Mike's comments and add more fuel to fire any possible local gossip, she forced a smile and got them back to the matter at hand.

'Now then, how are things going with you, Mike? How is your leg?'

'I've been doing all the exercises you gave me. Mostly the ankle is fine, although I do get some pain at times,' he admitted grudgingly.

Lauren nodded, knowing what a rough time Mike had been through and how important it was for him as a busy farmer to keep mobile and working. 'No doubt you've been overdo-ing things, though.'

'I've tried to increase my workload slowly, but I can't do as much as I'd like. There is still a bit of weakness and stiff-ness in the ankle.'

'That's to be expected,' she reminded him.

Lauren ran through some of the exercises and checked his range of movement. The offending leg bore the marks of the breaks and subsequent surgery he had sustained when part of a tree he had been cutting with a chainsaw had fallen on him, pinning him to the ground.

'Any problems from the bruised ribs?'

Mike shook his head. 'Not any more. The doctors tell me I healed quickly.'

'Just not quickly enough for you,' she filled in with an understanding smile. 'I know it seems a long haul, Mike, es-pecially when you're used to physical activity. You've done so well. We don't want any setbacks. Let your brother help you.'

'Joe's picked up enough of the slack. But you're not alone...Fran tells me I'm too impatient,' he conceded wryly, speaking of his wife with affection.

'Thankfully you didn't tear the ligaments, but the two frac-tures to your fibula—one above the ankle and one at the bottom, the lateral maleolus, where it joins the tibia—were serious. As you well know from your time in a cast after the operation to fit the plates and screws.' She gave him a sym-pathetic pat on the shoulder. 'You've worked hard to build up the strength in the muscles and to remobilise the joint. It must be frustrating, but keep up the exercises, don't try to do too much too soon, and you'll continue to improve.'

Mike nodded his agreement. 'Thanks, Lauren. I'll do my best. I've got so much to be grateful for.'

'You have indeed!' While he put his socks and shoes back

on, she reflected on how delighted the whole of Penhally had been at the news that Fran Trevellyan was expecting naturally after a previous miscarriage and an unsuccessful attempt at IVF. 'It's so exciting about the pregnancy. When is the baby due?'

'Late spring.' Mike positively glowed with joy. 'We're just praying everything goes without a hitch this time.'

'I'm sure it will,' she reassured him, happy for the couple.

'Things definitely seem different with this pregnancy. It's nearly November now, past the danger point in terms of the number of weeks when we lost the baby before. Kate is keeping a close eye on Fran and she says everything is fine.'

'So we have to make sure you are fit to run around changing nappies and chasing after an active toddler!' Lauren teased. 'Come back and see me in a month, Mike, but phone any time if you have questions, swelling or discomfort.'

After showing Mike out, she welcomed her next patient, a woman in her late forties who had presented with pain and associated symptoms in the C5 and C6 region of her neck. The classic 'poking-chin posture' evident at their first appointment had been caused by over-activity in the levetator scapulae and stermocleidomastoid muscles, along with a weakness of the cervical flexor muscles. This was Zena's third visit and she was showing excellent signs of improvement in her range of movement and her posture.

'The pain and stiffness are much less and I've had no more headaches or dizziness,' Zena reported, her relief evident. 'I'm finding the exercises easier now.'

'That's great.' Lauren was pleased that the combination of manipulation therapy she had used at the surgery and the corrective exercises Zena had done at home had resulted in the woman's progress. 'We'll make another appointment, but keep up the programme. It's helping correct your posture as well as increase your range of movement and strengthen the muscles.'

Happy that Zena was following her advice and had no more questions, Lauren sent her on her way and welcomed patient number three of the afternoon.

It turned out to be a busy Friday clinic, one that overran as she had a couple of new cases and time was needed to make a thorough assessment and take a complete history. Consequently it was late by the time she had finished her list. When her last patient had left, she sat down and adjusted her desk light so she could see more clearly to type up all her case notes and make comprehensive profiles of her new patients. She didn't anticipate being able to leave for home any time soon. Stifling a yawn with one hand, she switched on her computer and set to work, ignoring the noises coming from the workmen who were putting the finishing touches to alterations outside the building.

She was engrossed in updating her files when all the power suddenly went off, shutting down her computer and plunging her room into darkness. Losing any unsaved work was the least of her problems. Disoriented, she sat still, but her eyes didn't adjust to the gloom. She could see nothing. This was the realisation of one of her worst fears. Her heart started thudding under her ribs and she felt tense, her throat tightening. After sitting in the dark for a while, increasingly concerned, Lauren rose gingerly to her feet and, one hand extended out in front of her, slowly, awkwardly edged her way towards the door, thankful that her mental map of her new room was accurate. Judging each step with care, she found the door without bumping into anything, but opening it brought no relief.

It was pitch black throughout the whole surgery.

She strained to hear, but no sounds came. How late was it? Had everyone else gone home? She didn't recall hearing the workmen for a while. Pulling out her mobile phone, she tried to read the time on the screen, but the luminous glow provided scant light and failed to aid her vision. Increasingly alarmed, she pressed herself against the wall, not wanting to lose her bearings.

What should she do? Wait a bit to see what happened? Or call someone? She clutched her mobile phone tighter in her hand. How could she ring without alerting the person to her predicament? She wasn't ready to face the issue of her diminishing night vision herself, let alone confide in anyone else. Fear chilled her at the knowledge that she might not be able to ignore or hide the subtle but insidious changes to her sight for much longer.

A noise from upstairs made her jump. Her pulse throbbed.

'Hello?' Was that her voice sounding so uncharacteristically shaky and feeble? She hated this. What was happening to her? Silence descended again, enveloping her. Cursing herself for being feeble, battling the inner panic rising within her, she raised her voice. 'Is anyone there?'

Several moments later, footsteps sounded on the stairs. 'Lauren?'

'Gabriel!' Relief flooded through her and she blinked back a stupid threat of tears.

'Where are you, *chérie*?'

She pressed a hand to her chest, trying to calm her ragged breathing. 'Outside the physiotherapy room.'

'Stay there.' Gabriel's accented voice calmed her nerves. 'I'll find you.'

Seconds later, Lauren squinted at a pinpoint of light wavering in the darkness. Sensing Gabriel's nearness but misjudging the distance, she stepped out from the wall and bumped into his solid frame.

'Oomph!' she gasped.

His hands came out to steady her. 'Are you all right, Lauren?'

'Yes.' She was now. 'Thanks.'

It was brazen but she couldn't help snuggling closer, welcoming the feel of his arms coming around her. She absorbed his strength, scared of her lack of vision but unable to explain to him.

'I finished my surgery half an hour ago and Nick had just

called me up to the staffroom to talk about my first week when the power went off,' he explained, one hand soothing as it stroked up and down her spine.

'What's happened, do you think?'

'The contractors were finishing off some work outside and one of them cut a cable by mistake. Nick has gone to see them. I knew you were still here and was coming to find you when you called.'

Reassured by his presence and the knowledge he had thought of her, Lauren allowed herself to relax, some of the tension draining from her.

'Come and sit in my consulting room while we wait.'

'Um…' Lauren hesitated. Unfamiliar with the layout of his room, she didn't want to fall over anything or make even more of a fool of herself in front of him. How could he see with just a penlight? Had he guessed her problem? Not wanting to alert his suspicions by asking if they could just stand where they were, she reluctantly agreed to his suggestion. 'OK.'

His arm around her made her feel safe as he led her back down the corridor to the next doorway. Unable to see him, all her other senses seemed heightened, and his warmth wrapped around her like a comfort blanket in the dark. The citrusy male scent of him was familiar and exciting. Putting her trust in him, she was thankful that he guided her to a chair without any fuss. She sat down, disappointed when he released her. But then she heard the sounds of him dragging another chair closer, and he sat beside her, taking her hand in his, linking their fingers. She tried not to cling too tightly and reveal the extent of her unease.

'I want to thank you for all you have done helping me to fit in and making me welcome in Penhally,' he told her with warm sincerity.

'I don't think I'm responsible for much, but I'm glad that

you've settled so well. Word is you've made a great impression.' She wished there was enough light for her to see his face.

'I just want to be a good doctor for the people here,' he responded with simple but genuine modesty. 'Perhaps we can arrange a morning next week for me to come out on your home visits?'

'Yes, of course,' she agreed, delighted at the prospect.

Gabriel's thumb stroked across the inside of her wrist, making her shiver. 'Oliver and Chloe plan to go to Plymouth next weekend to see Rachel Kenner. Will you spend some time with me while they are gone? We can be alone…get to know one another better.'

'I'd like that.' Which was a massive understatement! She felt breathless with anticipation. The week ahead would be a long one…waiting. 'Gabriel—'

Before she could speak further, the lights flashed back on. Startled, Lauren blinked several times, her eyes taking a few moments to adjust and refocus. Then the fog cleared and Gabriel's gorgeous face swam clearly into view. She noticed his look of concern as he watched her, then he smiled, dimples creasing lean cheeks, and her stomach turned over.

'Lauren? Gabriel?' Nick's voice sounded from the front of the surgery.

With a wry grimace, Gabriel squeezed her fingers before he released her and stood up. Moving to the door, he called out to Nick, and a few moments later the older man arrived in the room.

'Here you both are.' Looking harassed, Nick ran a hand through his hair. 'I'm sorry about the disruption. I've been assured the problem is now resolved. Gabriel, perhaps we can have our informal debrief over a drink and something to eat?'

'Of course.' Gabriel's consent and smile were polite, but Lauren sensed his reluctance.

Nick turned to her. 'Are you heading home now, Lauren?'

'Yes, I am.' She could finish updating her computer files from her written notes another time, she decided, disappointed that she wouldn't be seeing Gabriel again this evening.

'Good. Right, then.' Nick rubbed his hands together and smiled. 'I'll meet you out front in a few moments.'

When he had gone, Lauren rose and walked towards the door, pausing to look at Gabriel. 'Thanks for being here.'

'No problem. If I don't catch up with you tomorrow, I'll see you at the football on Sunday.'

'All right.' She returned his smile, warmed through by the huskiness of his voice and the promise in his eyes. 'Goodnight, Gabriel.'

'Goodnight. Sleep well, *chérie.*'

After a short but tense and cautious drive, the lights of her cottage welcomed her home. The cars outside announced that both Oliver and Chloe were in, and she parked her own with extra care not to hit anything. As much as she loved her friends and valued their company, it was someone else who dominated her thoughts and whom she wished she was with right now.

Sleep well, Gabriel had said…

As had been the case every night since she had met him, she knew her sleep would be filled with dreams of a sexy Frenchman.

CHAPTER FOUR

SUNDAY dawned a perfect warm and sunny autumn day. The whole of Penhally had turned out to support the charity football match, along with many outsiders and autograph-hunters who had been drawn by the impressive number of sporting and television personalities in attendance. The media were also out in force, capturing the action from the school playing fields. Given the size of the crowd, plus the interest in the snap auction of items donated by the celebrities, there was going to be a very healthy sum of money added to the relief fund.

Kate didn't want to think about the flood. Almost three weeks on and the memories of being stuck in an upstairs flat in Bridge Street with Nick, the water rising beneath them, still left her feeling shaky. They had struggled successfully to deliver Stephanie Richards's breech baby, and then had come the frightening experience of being winched up to the rescue helicopter. Kate shivered despite the mild temperature.

'Are you all right, Mum?'

'Yes, my love. I'm fine.' Smiling, she ruffled Jem's hair. He'd found her at half-time and was taking advantage of the refreshments she'd brought. 'Are you enjoying yourself?'

'It's cool! I've got some great autographs,' he added, pointing to all the signatures he'd collected on his football jersey, then his eyes went round in alarm. 'You won't wash them off, will you?'

'Never, I promise.' She hid her amusement as she reassured him, watching as he drained his fruit drink and wiped the back of his hand across his mouth.

'It was good of Uncle Nick to arrange for me be a ballboy.'

Uncle Nick. Pain lanced through her. Jem had no idea that Nick was his natural father. Would the man she had loved for ever one day claim his son? Or were old hurts and the weight of guilt too much to be overcome? While they had been trapped during the flood, they had talked about that long-ago night when they had lost their heads…a night of great stress and emotion that had resulted in Jem's conception. Nick had promised to try to make an effort to come to terms with the situation, and at least be more attentive to Jem, even if he couldn't go as far as making a public declaration of fatherhood. Kate wasn't holding her breath that anything would come of it but she could not help but hope—for Jem's sake if not her own. So far Nick had kept his word and things were less tense between them.

'The second half is starting soon. Will you come and watch me?' Jem asked, returning after throwing the empty drink carton into a nearby litter bin.

'Of course, my love.'

He caught her hand and tugged. 'Come on, then.'

Kate allowed her son to lead her towards the touchline, pleased that he was so happy. Nick had already returned from the half-time break, acting as team doctor for the celebrity side. Jem released her hand and ran to him. Kate saw Nick's guarded smile as he greeted the boy and heard the modulated tones of his voice.

'Back to help again?' he asked, and Jem nodded enthusiastically. 'Good lad.'

Sharing a look with the most enigmatic of men, Kate

mouthed, 'Thank you,' understanding how difficult it was for Nick to confront his own demons. Not wanting to push things or make a scene in public, she saw Lauren and Chloe returning to the side of the pitch and went to join them.

'Everything OK, Kate?' Chloe asked.

She nodded in response to the gentle query, seeing the understanding in the younger woman's green eyes. Her fellow midwife was one of only two other people, besides herself and Nick, who knew the secret about the identity of Jem's father.

'It's been an excellent day and Jem is having fun being part of it.' Again, Kate's gaze strayed to where her son waited impatiently for the game to restart. Nick was watching him, too, and she wondered what was going through his mind. Aware she was on dangerous ground, she turned her attention back to her two colleagues. 'Oliver did a brilliant job organising this. It's a huge success.'

Chloe glowed with pleasure at the praise for her fiancé. 'I know. He worked so hard. Jack Tremayne helped, too. Both of them were able to call in favours from their days in London, securing the support of several national celebrities as well as the Cornish ones.'

'Everyone's really got behind the event,' Lauren added with approval. 'Despite the arrival of his baby boy, Dragan worked hard behind the scenes for today.'

'I think he would have liked to play, but it's understandable that he and Melinda wanted to keep out of public view after the press intrusions last spring,' Chloe pointed out, and Kate nodded in agreement, remembering what it had been like in the village when Melinda had been identified as a member of European royalty.

As both sets of players jogged out for the second half, cheers echoed around the playing fields.

'Gabriel has been a star, jumping in to give support the

moment he arrived here,' Kate commented, glancing at Lauren. 'He scored an excellent goal, too.'

'All our guys have been great.'

Kate smiled at Lauren's reply, noting the wink Gabriel sent the young physiotherapist as he ran past and the flush that warmed her cheeks in response. It was clear where those two were heading! And Kate couldn't be more pleased for them. Her smile broadened as Oliver detoured to give Chloe a kiss. Leaving the two friends to focus on the match—and the men who held their interest—Kate wandered farther along the side of the pitch so she could keep a better eye on Jem.

The flood had been terrible for the whole village, causing physical and emotional trauma. The damage to property would take many months to overcome, while the loss of Audrey Baxter and Reverend Kenner was a tragedy never to be forgotten. But the aftermath, including the mass support for today's event, showed what could happen when the community pulled together.

Penhally's previous disaster, the big storm a decade ago, had been the catalyst that had caused the moment of madness between herself and Nick which had led to Jem's existence. Maybe the flood could have done some good if it sparked a turning point for the future...if Nick found a way to move on from the past and accept his son.

'You really like Gabriel, don't you?' Chloe asked Lauren as Kate walked away from them.

Lauren nodded, although 'like' was an insipid word to describe the complexity of her feelings and the extent of her attraction. 'I do.'

'The electricity the two of you generate when you're together could power the whole of Cornwall,' her friend proclaimed, giving her a quick hug. 'I hope everything works out. I want you to be as happy as I am—and around Gabriel you look how I feel when I'm with Oliver.' She hesitated a moment, then added more soberly, 'I know we rarely mention it, but I'll never forget all you've done for me, Lauren.'

Chloe was such a sweetheart. That she was now blossoming was wonderful. Lauren still vividly recalled the state in which she had found Chloe eleven and a half years ago when the girl, then sixteen, had been beaten by her father. She had helped Chloe get away that night and was so proud of the success she had gone on to make of her life. Even so, for a long while Chloe had shut herself off from love because of her past—until Oliver had arrived. The perfect man to be understanding, gentle and loving, he'd taught Chloe all about being a woman in the fullest sense of the word.

'You've come such a long way and I'm so delighted for you,' she said, hugging Chloe back.

'Thank you. Ooh, sorry, I didn't mean to get all sentimental!' Chloe's smile was wobbly, her eyes bright with a suspicion of tears. Doggedly, she changed the subject. 'Can you believe Vicky taking off like that after the flood?'

Lauren had been friends with Vicky Clements since junior school. They were close but she acknowledged Vicky's faults—primary amongst them being her propensity for gossip. Vicky didn't mean any harm, but she often hurt people's feelings and said thoughtless things she shouldn't. And working at her mother's hair and beauty salon, Vicky heard a lot of tales she was only too keen to pass on. They'd had a lot of fun together over the years, and Lauren enjoyed the flighty woman's company, but it was to Chloe that Lauren turned for advice and to share confidences. Chloe was discreet and kind and totally selfless.

'It will be a while until the salon is up and running again after the flood damage. Vicky's mother is going to keep up her regular clients by doing home visits until the salon can reopen,' she explained now. 'Vicky's been restless since embarking on her hot new romance with the guitarist of that up-and-coming band she met in a nightclub in Rock. When the band asked her to go with them on their world tour, to do all the styling and hair for them and the backing singers, she felt it was too good an opportunity to miss.'

'A real adventure, for sure,' Chloe agreed.

'Vicky's never been so committed to a man before...maybe this will change her.'

'It'll seem quiet around here with her gone.' A twinkle of mischief appeared in her friend's green eyes. 'At least Vicky is too busy with her own love life to gossip about or inter-fere in ours!'

'Amen to that.'

Lauren remembered how Vicky's tactless meddling had caused problems—thankfully temporary ones—for Chloe and Oliver back in the summer. It was a good thing that Vicky was away for the next few months, she decided. She didn't need her nosy friend making wisecracks or involving herself in what Lauren hoped was her own budding new relationship with a certain sexy French doctor.

'The second half is about to start.' Chloe's comment drew Lauren from her thoughts. 'It's been competitive but friendly so far—I hope no one gets hurt.'

'Me, too.'

The famous, top-flight referee, who had agreed to officiate for the charity match, blew his whistle and the game began again in earnest with the celebrities leading the locals by four goals to three. Lauren, as Penhally team physio, was kept busy as the game went on, with various muscle pulls and a couple of sprains. Then Jack Tremayne received a nasty cut to his knee, one that was suspiciously shaped like a stud mark from a misplaced football boot.

'You need stitches in this,' Adam Donnelly declared, ex-amining the wound and stemming the bleeding.

'It can wait until after the game.' Jack ignored the combined medical opinion and insisted on rejoining the fray once he had been bandaged up. 'If we win, I'll let you at me with a needle.'

Adam turned away with a good-natured grin. 'Gee, thanks. Perhaps I'll misplace the local anaesthetic. That or sew your lips together,' he called back, making everyone laugh.

The game continued and the goals kept coming for both sides. Lauren cheered loudest of all when Gabriel scored another spectacular goal to put the home team in the lead with only ten minutes left to play. Standing on the sidelines, enjoying the action, she couldn't stop watching Gabriel. He had a wonderful physique, strong but leanly athletic, and his sleeveless top—part of the players' kit donated by a national sportswear chain for the occasion—showed off the roped, corded muscles of his arms to perfection. Oliver had a good body, too, but looking at him did nothing for her in terms of attraction. Neither did any of the other men here. Only Gabriel. Just one sight of him stole her breath and set a fire of need smouldering inside her, clenching her stomach and leaving her giddy with excited anticipation.

Watching him so closely, she was aware the instant something went wrong. She was already reaching for her bag when Gabriel collapsed as if he had been poleaxed. Seeing him fall scared her witless. Then she was running towards him, even before the referee had given her permission to cross the pitch. Gabriel needed her. Her heart in her mouth, Lauren dropped to her knees beside the prone figure on the ground.

'Gabe, what's wrong?' Her voice shook with emotion and she didn't consciously realise she had shortened his name. 'Where are you hurt?'

'Cramp,' he managed through teeth gritted with pain.

His right leg was rigid with vicious spasms. Lauren got to her feet and grasped his ankle, holding his leg up straight and pushing back against his foot to try to ease the locked muscles. By the time the referee, Oliver and a few of the other Penhally players had jogged across to see what was going on, some of the knotted tension in Gabriel's leg was beginning to dissipate.

'You'll have to carry out any other treatment off the pitch,' the referee insisted, for all the world like this was a major professional match rather than a fundraising one.

'I can play on,' Gabriel insisted, trying to get to his feet. 'There's not much longer to go. I want to see it out.'

Lauren held on to him as he took a few faltering steps only for his leg to give out and cramp up again. 'Gabe, you can't. We need to get you rehydrated and your leg dealt with.'

'She's right, my friend.' As Oliver backed her up, she sent him a grateful smile. 'Let Lauren take care of you.'

'You've given your all and scored two goals,' she reminded him.

Coffee-coloured eyes, threaded with pain, looked into hers. After a moment, he nodded. 'All right.'

'Thank you.' She turned to Oliver. 'I'll take him down to the treatment room.'

'Good idea. We'll ferry down any other walking wounded when we're done.'

As Oliver went to organise a substitute for the last part of the game, Lauren grabbed her bag with one hand and slid her free arm around Gabriel's waist, helping him balance as he limped to the sidelines. He put an arm around her shoulders, accepting the support, and she welcomed the weight of it. Even given the circumstances, she couldn't help but be aware of how it felt to be so close. She could feel the heat of him and scent his earthy maleness.

Chloe and Kate awaited them on the touchline, looking worried.

'Is there anything we can do?' Kate asked.

'Can you keep an eye on him while I get my car?' She hated to leave him but no way could he walk all the way to the car park. 'If you have water or a sports drink, Gabriel needs them.'

'Of course.'

Knowing Gabriel was being cared for, Lauren ran for the car. Soon she was driving as close as she could to the pitch, pleased to find that Chloe and Kate had helped to guide Gabriel to her through the crowds. She jumped out and hurried round to open the passenger door, noting the tension on his face as his leg tightened again when he sat in the restricted space.

'Thanks.' She smiled at her friends and slid back behind the wheel, grateful it was only a very short distance to the surgery.

She threw him a quick glance, pleased to see he was continuing to drink. His eyes were closed and he was stretching out his leg as much as the confines of the car would allow. 'Are you OK?'

'I'm getting too old for this,' he joked. 'Don't worry, *chérie*, the cramp will ease.'

It certainly would once she had a chance to work on those calf and thigh muscles. But she made no comment as she parked outside the surgery, unlocked the door and helped Gabriel inside. The problem with her plan only hit her once they were in the physio room.

Alone.

And Gabriel had gone behind the curtain to take off his football boots, socks and shorts.

Oh, sweet mercy.

Now he was lying face down on the treatment table. True, he was still wearing his football top but the towel covering his lower half reminded her of the day they had met. Lauren swallowed. She was a professional. She could do this. She could put hands on Gabriel's scrumptious body and give him a therapeutic massage without thinking about or acting on any of the salacious and erotic fantasies running through her mind.

Of course she could. And would. If she kept telling herself enough, she might even believe it.

Ignoring the way her hands were shaking, she took out a bottle of the embrocation she favoured for working on tired, cramped muscles and approached the table. Biting her lip, she pushed the hem of the towel up to mid-thigh. His legs were beautifully sculpted, all toned muscle and supple, dark skin.

'L-let's get these knots sorted out,' she murmured, cursing her lack of control. 'Ready?'

'Do your worst, Lauren.'

'Right.'

She poured oil into her hands and rubbed them together to warm it, telling herself to forget all the 'worst' things she really wanted to do to him and focus on the professional massage. Sucking in a steadying breath, she touched him for the first time. Her hands settled low on his calf, feeling the tightness of the muscles in spasm as she pressed upwards with deft strokes to the back of the knee. She forced herself to concentrate on what she was doing. She couldn't allow herself to dwell on how wonderful it was to touch him, or let her gaze to move any farther up to where the towel brushed his thighs and draped across the enticing shape of his rear.

Gabriel groaned as her thumbs circled deeply into his flesh. '*Mon Dieu*, that feels good.'

The sultry roughness of his voice shimmered to every nerve ending. *He* certainly felt good, his skin warm and male beneath her fingers. She worked slowly up his leg, relaxing the muscles of the calf and thigh, feeling his tension ease while her own magnified. No matter how hard she tried to remain professional, to keep her touch neutral and impersonal, she had never been so intensely aware in her life. She wanted this man as she had never wanted anyone before. The temptation to caress, to glide her hands higher and allow her fingers to explore his body was overwhelming.

Lauren was relieved that Gabriel didn't talk. She didn't think she could. Indeed, he seemed unaffected, his head turned to one side, resting on his crossed forearms. His eyes were closed, and he gave every impression of being relaxed and at ease, while she was on red alert, aroused and aching. It was mortifying.

'Turn over now, please,' she directed, injecting as much calm unconcern into her voice as she could manage.

'Lauren…'

She reached for the bottle of oil. 'Hmm?'

'I think it is fine now, *chérie*,' he stated, sounding oddly wary.

'Nonsense,' she riposted briskly. If he could do this without batting an eyelid, so could she. 'I haven't finished massaging the leg.'

'But—'

'Please, Gabriel.'

He huffed out a breath, and she frowned, wondering what the problem was as he continued to hesitate. She waited endless moments before he slowly rolled over. Her pulse rate rocketed and her throat closed as the reason for his reticence became apparent…the tented towel gave evidence to the fact that the extent of his arousal matched her own. She couldn't look away. Her stomach knotted with an ache of need, her heart pounded, and she could feel her nipples pucker even further in response, sensitive against the lacy fabric of her bra.

Gabriel sat up and swung his legs off the table. 'Lauren.' His hands cupped her face, raising it until she was looking into eyes so dark and hot with desire she felt singed from the fire.

'Gabe…'

His name had barely whispered from her lips before his mouth met hers, firm, demanding, delicious. The plastic bottle she was holding fell forgotten to the floor, her fingers trailing up the leanly muscled contours of his arms before clinging to the strength of his shoulders. She had longed for this moment.

Had yearned to taste him. And now, at last, she was. There
was no hesitancy, no awkwardness of a first kiss. It was as if
their mouths, their bodies, already knew each other.

Her lips parted in welcome and she moaned as he accepted
the invitation with barely restrained hunger, sweeping inside,
taking and giving, stroking and sliding. One arm wrapped
around her waist, pulling her closer, and she stepped up
between his thighs. The fingers of his other hand sank into her
hair, tilting the angle of her head to deepen the contact
between them. His touch was electric, his kiss explosive.
Lauren felt as if all the cells and molecules in her body bonded
with his, their genes homing in on each other.

The kiss melted her, stealing her reason. Her legs threatened to give way and she tightened her hold, leaning into him
for support. She had never felt like this before. The intense,
thorough kiss was even more than she had imagined and
dreamed about in the time she had known him. She met and
matched Gabriel's every move, never wanting this to end.
Her tongue twined with his, and she sucked on him, excited
when he nibbled at her lips, teasing and tormenting before
deepening the kiss again and sucking back at her. She wanted
more, needed everything, revelled in his immediate response,
the passion between them intensifying.

Gabriel lost himself in the sweet heat of Lauren's kiss. The
firm softness of her breasts pressed against his chest and he
could feel the hardened crests of her aroused nipples through
the thin barrier of their clothes. His hand grazed down her
back to cup the enticing swell of her rear, and he shaped her,
pulling her tighter, swallowing her involuntary whimper as she
met the fullness of his erection. An answering groan escaped
him as she wriggled closer, rubbing herself against him.

He'd never felt this out of control from a kiss, but the wild
chemistry between them had him on the ragged edge already.

A kiss was never going to be enough. He wanted her. Wanted her as he had never wanted any other woman in his life. Needed to see her and touch her and taste her all over. Couldn't wait to unite their bodies, to possess her fully, to lose himself deep and tight inside her. Lauren and this incredible passion they shared could make him forget all about the problems awaiting him back in France.

A loud knock on the door brought them sharply back to reality. They broke apart, panting for breath. How could he have forgotten where they were? Lauren's eyes opened, dark grey and smoky with unfulfilled passion, her regret at the interruption matching his own. They stared at each other and he watched as she stepped back a pace, raising shaky fingers to lips that were moist and plump from the incendiary kiss that had taken him to paradise. He could see the pulse beating wildly at her throat, mimicking the way his own heart pounded a frantic rhythm beneath his ribs.

'*Damnez-le,*' he cursed, drawing in a ragged breath. 'Wrong time, wrong place.'

'Yes. Gabe…'

No one had ever shortened his name before. He liked it. Liked it that Lauren was the only one who used it, who spoke it with such husky intimacy. Renewed heat prickled through him as they looked at each other, her eyes dark with an answering desire and need. Another knock at the door had Lauren moving farther away, adjusting her clothes and smoothing down the hair he had tousled.

'Just a minute,' she called out, her voice sounding shaky and rough.

He licked his lips, still able to taste her. Her subtle sweet-pea scent had invaded him, familiar, arousing, sensual. His whole body was charged with excitement. There was bitter disappointment that they'd had to stop, yet raging anticipation at the thought of how explosive the experience of making love was going to be for them when the time came. As it inevitably would.

'I'd better get that.' She forced the words out but they sounded hoarse.

Knowing he couldn't delay things now, Gabriel sighed. 'I know.'

He retreated behind the curtain, listening as she opened the door and had a conversation with Adam.

'Sorry to bother you, Lauren. I hope Gabriel's OK. We've brought down two more team players needing treatment,' Adam explained. 'I'm just going to stitch Jack's cut—we won, so I'm at him with the needle!—and Dan Somers has pulled his hamstring. It looks a bad one so he's going to need follow-up treatment. Can you see what you can do for him?'

'Of course.'

Gabriel heard the thread of reluctance at being interrupted mingle with genuine concern in her voice as she agreed. The son of one of the local farmers, Dan had played for the Penhally team and Gabriel had met him for the first time that day. Hurrying so as not to embarrass Lauren in any way, Gabriel pulled on his shorts then sat down to sort out his socks and football boots. Once he was done, he drew back the curtain in time to see Lauren glance over her shoulder at him, her expression flustered.

'We're just about finished here,' she told Adam. 'Give me a few moments to make sure Gabriel is all right and I'll be happy to help Dan.'

'Thanks, Lauren. He's in the waiting room. We'll help him through.'

When Adam had gone, Gabriel moved up behind her and, hidden by the door, turned her to face him, cupping her cheek with one palm, enjoying the feel of her warm, soft skin.

'I'm sorry,' she whispered, and it was an effort to drag his gaze away from the temptation of her mouth.

'It's not your fault. Next weekend we'll have some privacy. I don't want to rush things and have to steal odd moments like this.' He felt the tremor run through her in response to his words. 'Thank you for making my leg feel so much better.'

Her smile held a spark of mischief and he chuckled, not sure if it was the expert massage or the fiery kiss that had most eased the pain in his cramping leg. Hearing people approaching along the corridor, Gabriel released her and stepped back, allowing her to open the door again so that Adam and Oliver could assist Dan Somers into the room.

'How are you feeling Gabriel?' Oliver asked as Lauren and Adam settled Dan on the treatment table.

'Like a new man, thanks to Lauren.'

Gabriel noticed the warmth bloom on Lauren's cheeks as she rejoined them. 'He should be fine,' she said.

'I'm heading home with Chloe,' Oliver continued, apparently oblivious to the charged atmosphere. 'Do you want a lift as Lauren's going to be busy for a while?'

'Sure. Thanks, Oliver.'

'Thank *you* for all your help. The match was a huge success. And we won—thanks to our secret weapon in our French star!' Oliver smiled, his humour infectious.

'We'll leave you to get on, Lauren,' Adam decreed. 'I have an appointment with Jack and a needle!'

Lauren walked them to the door, and Gabriel hung back, allowing Adam and Oliver to leave ahead of him. He paused, leaning in to whisper in her ear. 'Later, *chérie*. Next weekend we'll have time for us,' he promised, gratified by the flare of desire in her eyes.

Filled with impatience at the wait and disappointed to be leaving her, Gabriel walked away. The time until they could be alone together with no threat of interruptions couldn't come soon enough.

* * *

The frustration and anticipation was every bit as bad as he expected as the following week unfolded and he had little time alone with Lauren. One bright spot on the horizon was the arrangement to spend a morning accompanying her on her home visits. He was happy to give up his time off on Thursday because it meant being with her.

Finally it was Wednesday. His late-afternoon surgery was typically mixed, with cases including a young man with psoriasis, a fifty-two-year-old woman with menopausal symptoms, a teenage girl with a nasty stye, who needed some antibiotic eyedrops, an elderly man with signs of blood in his urine, who needed further tests to rule out infection and determine the source of the bleeding, a toddler with earache and several cases of colds, sore throats and influenza.

'You done for the day?' Oliver asked, tapping on the open consulting-room door and stepping inside.

'Yes.' Gabriel smiled, waving Oliver to a chair and saving the notes he had written up on his computer to back up his handwritten ones. 'What can I do for you?'

'I hear you are going out on home visits with Lauren tomorrow.'

And the time couldn't come soon enough, Gabriel thought, nodding at his friend. 'That's right.'

'You'll be visiting one of our regular patients, Gertrude Stanbury. She's quite a character, as I am sure Lauren will explain to you!' With a bad-boy smile, Oliver sat back in the chair and hooked one ankle over the opposite knee. 'Would you mind giving her a flu jab? I found out today that the district nurses missed her off their schedule by mistake, and I'm not due to see her for a fortnight. I don't want her to wait that long. I'd go myself, but I have a full list tomorrow and I'm off on Friday. I could get one of the nurses to fit her in, but as you'll be there anyway…'

'No problem, Oliver.'

'Great. Thanks. Chloe's free on Friday, too, so we're planning to get off early for our weekend in Plymouth.'

'I hope Rachel Kenner is coping.' Having heard the full story of how the troublesome youth Gary Lovelace had targeted the vicar's daughter so cruelly, he felt sad for the girl. 'I'm sure she will be delighted to see you.'

Concern shadowed Oliver's expression. 'Chloe is fretting about her. It will set our minds at rest if she's settled in as happily as possible with her aunt and uncle, as well as managing her pregnancy. Goodness knows how she is dealing with all that on top of losing her father.'

'Grief affects people in different ways.' Realising that his tone of voice had revealed more than he had intended and had roused Oliver's interest, Gabriel cleared his throat and changed the subject, unwilling to think of home and family. 'Don't worry about anything here. I'll see to Ms Stanbury's flu vaccination tomorrow. And I know Lauren will take care of the cats for Chloe while you are gone.'

A knowing gleam shone in Oliver's dark eyes. 'Somehow I doubt that you and Lauren will be sorry to have us out of the way for a while. We've cramped your style a bit, having to move into Gatehouse Cottage after the flood.'

'It's fine.'

'You look much more relaxed than when you first arrived,' Oliver continued after a moment.

Gabriel nodded. 'I feel it. It's been enjoyable and I've learned a great deal. I'm glad I came here.'

'Moving to Penhally Bay certainly changed *my* life.'

'How so?' he prompted, interested to know more about the man who had become a close friend in such a short time.

'I was dissatisfied with my life in London and knew I wanted something different. I'd planned to take time to settle in and establish myself before I started thinking about the future and a family. But then I met Chloe. I knew from the first moment that she was the one for me.' He glanced across with a smile that was both reminiscent and wicked. 'It took me a while to acknowledge the truth of it to myself—and a bit longer to persuade Chloe I was serious. She's the best thing that's ever happened to me. I've never been this contented.'

'I'm pleased for you. Anyone can see how great you are as a couple.'

'I hope Penhally will bring you the same contentment.'

Gabriel hesitated a moment, finding it surprisingly easy to share confidences with Oliver—something that was uncharacteristic for him. 'I have issues to work out from home... things to consider about my future. And a year here in which to decide on the direction of my life.'

'Penhally is a good place to think. If you want to talk, I'm here. And there's Lauren,' he added, a teasing glint in his eyes. 'The sparks between you are obvious. I hope you'll find your time in Cornwall brings you the same happiness and direction it gave to me.'

'Thank you, *mon ami*.'

Gabriel wondered the same thing. Would his time in Penhally not only lead him to some answers about his family dilemma but also open up a whole new world of opportunity with Lauren? Their friendship had established and deepened from the first moment. It had happened quickly, but there was no denying the connection between them. The heightened awareness and desire fizzing through him whenever he so much as thought of Lauren could not be ignored.

He was looking forward to finding out what the next weeks and months held in store for him.

CHAPTER FIVE

'WE JUST have Gertrude Stanbury left to visit,' Lauren informed Gabriel as she steered the car away from the Mitchell family's home and headed towards Trelissa Road.

Despite hearing good things from others, this morning was the first time she had seen Gabriel in action as a doctor for herself. She was even more impressed than she had anticipated. He had an innate warmth that set people at their ease and evoked their trust. He was interested and genuine, compassionate without being patronising. Combined with everything else she knew about him, it made her admire and care about him even more.

'Paul Mitchell is an inspiring youngster,' Gabriel said, and Lauren smiled.

'He is. I always feel humbled by his bravery,' she admitted, shaking her head at the way the eleven-year-old coped with the limits Duchenne muscular dystrophy placed on his life. 'Paul's faced each new challenge and stage of the disease with good humour and fortitude, although he hates having to use the wheelchair now. He loves school but doesn't attend full time because of the difficulties, so has some lessons at home, like today. Thankfully he's a genius with a computer…it's his pride and joy. The family don't have much materially but they do all they can to meet Paul's needs with home adaptations and equipment. They are very close and wonderfully supportive of each other, not to mention grateful for whatever back-up we can give them.'

Gabriel nodded, his admiration evident. 'They are certainly devoted to Paul and take his exercise regime seriously.'

'Paul's willingness to keep trying, to do the stretching exercises for his muscles and the breathing ones to keep his lungs clear, expel the mucus and reduce the risk of infections, makes my job much easier. He's determined not to let it beat him. And we are all determined to work as a team to ensure that Paul has the fullest and most enjoyable life possible.'

'I think you are amazing.' Gabriel's compliment warmed her inside. 'I've seen you today helping a variety of people—Harry Biscombe with his osteoporosis, Edith Jones with her minor stroke, the after-effects of her broken knee and assorted health problems, Stella Chamberlain with her onset of Parkinson's disease, the Morrisons with young baby Timmy's cystic fibrosis, and now Paul.' He paused and she could feel his gaze on her. 'You have a special rapport with your patients, Lauren. You give so much of yourself. It's not just a job to you.'

His praise touched her, his opinion mattering a great deal. But his own dedication and giftedness as a doctor was unsurpassed. 'You're the same. Medicine—caring for people in need—is part of the very fabric of who you are.'

'Yes.'

There was a thread of sadness and confusion in his voice, along with a weary sigh. She glanced at him, wondering what lay behind his change of tone. Did it have something to do with why he had been so keen to leave France? There was so much she wanted to discover about this man.

'Gabriel—'

'Tell me about Gertrude Stanbury,' he suggested, interrupting her. 'Oliver tells me she is something of a character.'

Reluctantly, Lauren allowed the change of subject...for

now. 'You can say that again. Gertrude is retired now but she was an institution as long-time headmistress at the secondary school here in Penhally. She has a bungalow in Gull Close and suffers badly from arthritis, especially in the knees and hands, although other joints are becoming affected more seriously. She had her first knee replacement recently but is still not very mobile. Her recovery wasn't helped by the flood, but at least she was safe. Thankfully one of the young local girls, Tassie Lovelace, was visiting her at the time, and as the water started coming in she was able to encourage Gertrude into the attic, from where they were rescued by one of the helicopter crews.'

'How on earth did Gertrude manage to get up there?'

'I've no idea, but it didn't do her joints much good.' Lauren shook her head, pausing a moment as she parked in Trelissa Road, taking extra care to make sure she didn't have a repeat of reversing into anything…not with Gabriel as a witness. 'Until her home is fit to live in again, Dr Tom Cornish has insisted she live in this house—it used to belong to his father and Tom inherited it. A former Penhally resident, he happened to be here, dealing with the house, when the flood hit. He's head of Deltaron, the international rescue agency, and his team were marvellous during the emergency.'

Gabriel unclipped his seat belt and glanced at the house. 'Why would Dr Cornish loan Gertrude his house?'

'Apparently Tom was a bit wild when he was young and, although a formidable adversary, Gertrude always believed in him. Tom was glad to help her now and repay her faith in him.' She chuckled at her own memories of the feisty woman who had watched over the school and its pupils with an all-seeing eye. 'She scared the life out of most of us!'

'I shall look forward to hearing all about your misspent youth!'

Lauren laughed. 'The trouble is, Gertrude will be all too keen to tell you.'

'Now I'm even more intrigued.' He smiled back at her, and she felt the faint wash of pink that tinged her cheeks.

'Just don't believe everything you hear.'

'Maybe that depends what *everything* is.'

His teasing deepened her blush. She was aware of him following close behind as she walked towards the house and opened the front door with the spare key they kept at the surgery. Rotund, white-haired Gertrude was propped up on pillows in a comfortable recliner in the living room. Age and crippling arthritis had brought an end to her working life, but had done nothing to dim the sharp expression in her steely grey gaze or take the edge off her shrewd watchfulness. A sense of humour and keen interest still lurked behind her outward bark and bluster.

'Oh, it's you, Lauren. Come in, then, if I have to be poked and prodded,' she grumbled, a sparkle dancing in her eyes as she took her first look at Gabriel. 'Who is this handsome creature?'

'I've brought Dr Devereux to meet you, Ms Stanbury.'

Lauren introduced them and watched with amusement as the elderly lady regally extended her hand, a pink glow washing pale, papery cheeks at Gabriel's gallant greeting. She was surprised, however, when Gertrude began speaking rapidly to him in his own language.

'I'd forgotten that you used to teach French, Ms Stanbury.'

'I did have a life before becoming a headmistress, you know,' she barked in response.

Lauren saw the laughter in Gabriel's eyes and struggled to contain a giggle. 'How have you been since I last saw you? Have you been managing the exercises I gave you?'

'Pure torture, they are.'

'I'm sorry to hear that.' Lauren smiled, not fooled for a moment by Gertrude's mock complaints. As she carried out a gentle examination and encouraged her to try a few more movements and exercises, both standing and sitting, she could see the improvement in the knee that had been replaced. 'You are doing so well, Ms Stanbury. Once your other knee is done, you'll find your mobility will be much better. How are your hands? Are you finding the new combination of pills Dr Oliver put you on helping at all?'

An affectionate expression crossed the elderly lady's face at the mention of Oliver, for whom it was well-known she had a soft spot. 'These pills are an improvement.'

'I'm so glad. We'll run through a few more gentle exercises to keep you moving, then Dr Devereux is going to see to your flu jab.'

A groan greeted the news and Lauren shared another smile with Gabriel. When she had finished, she sat back on her heels and packed away her things while Gabriel dealt with the vaccination and chatted with Gertrude in French. Lauren didn't catch much of the conversation, but hearing the names of Martin and her parents mentioned, she smothered a groan of her own. Maybe it was a good thing she couldn't remember much of her schoolgirl French or she would likely be mortified at whatever Gertrude was telling Gabriel. The former headmistress possessed an encyclopaedic knowledge about her past students and embarrassing moments were recounted with glee. Feeling Gabriel watching her, she looked up. The interested speculation evident in his mocha-brown eyes made her wonder what questions she would face once they were alone.

'You didn't understand much of that, did you, Lauren? You would remember your French had *I* been your teacher,' Ms Stanbury rebuked, reverting to English, mischief in her eyes. 'As I recall, it was always art and sport with you. When you weren't tripping over and dropping things. Still,' her tormentor continued, her knowing gaze moving from Lauren to Gabriel and back again, 'it seems to me that your interest in things French has increased considerably of late.'

As Gabriel chuckled, Lauren fought another blush. The

woman was a menace! Fortunately, they were soon able to escape. Unfortunately, her time with Gabriel was over for today and she dropped him back at the Manor House.

'Gertrude Stanbury was everything I expected and more,' he teased, silencing her grunt of disgust with a parting kiss that left her breathless. He drew back and stroked the fingers of one hand down her cheek. 'Thank you for this morning, *chérie*. I learned a lot.' Lauren feared he had learned rather more than she had intended, thanks to Gertrude's runaway tongue. 'We'll talk at the weekend.'

With his enigmatic promise ringing in her ears, Lauren returned to the surgery for her afternoon list of appointments, wondering what the weekend held in store and if, once finally alone, they would succumb to the charge of desire that hummed between them.

Today had been his most enjoyable day in Cornwall so far, Gabriel reflected, lingering over coffee after the meal he had cooked and shared with Lauren in the kitchen at the Manor House on Saturday evening.

The weather had continued to be kind and they had spent the day exploring, Lauren showing him Bodmin Moor and parts of the coast. They had also indulged in a number of increasingly heated kisses that had whetted his appetite for more. From the look in her eyes and the responses of her body, he was pretty sure Lauren felt the same. Foxy had accompanied them on their walks, growing in confidence all the time, and the sleek greyhound now lay asleep in the basket Lauren had brought up for him. Returning from their outing as dusk had descended, they had stopped off at Gatehouse Cottage to check on and feed Chloe's cats.

He had noticed once again Lauren's nervousness and caution in the dark, the care she took, the way she sometimes counted to herself as if she was measuring her steps because she couldn't see. He wasn't even sure she was aware of the habit. Once the lights went on, she reverted to her usual self. Again, her actions puzzled and concerned him, but he was wary of mentioning anything to her until he had a clearer idea if there was, indeed, anything wrong…and until she knew him well enough to trust him. Was he making something out of nothing? Maybe, if everyone else accepted her as clumsy and she had always been this way, he was seeing something that wasn't there and Lauren just had bad night vision. Gertrude Stanbury had confirmed Lauren had been renowned for being accident prone even in her schooldays. He planned to keep a watch on her until he was more certain of the facts.

Looking at Lauren now, Gabriel marvelled again at her natural beauty. Her skin glowed with freshness, her hair, left loose around her shoulders, shone with life—myriad shades of light browns and golds—and her womanly figure was shown off to perfection in dark jeans and a lilac button-through top that hugged the fullness of her breasts. Long, sooty lashes rose and beautiful grey eyes stared into his own.

'What?' she asked, her voice husky, rosy lips parting slightly as her tongue-tip peeped out to moisten them, tightening his gut with need.

He edged his chair closer and reached out to take one of her hands in both of his, holding her palm up in one hand and stroking her soft skin with the fingers of the other, feeling the way her flesh quivered in response to his touch.

'I had a great time today, Lauren.'

'Me, too.'

He forced himself to look away from the temptation of her mouth for the moment. They had talked about so much today but had not touched on any of the things that were contentious or difficult, like family and past relationships. Gabriel thought of all the well-meaning but meddling gossip Gertrude had told him on Thursday. Knowing how he felt about having his own privacy invaded, he didn't want to pressure Lauren, yet he knew they had reached a point where an exchange of confidences was needed if they were to take the simmering passion that only grew hotter and more intense between them to its logical conclusion.

'Will you tell me about Martin?' he asked after a long moment of silence. He watched Lauren carefully but saw nothing in her reaction to worry him, no sign she was still in love with the man Gertrude had mentioned.

'Martin and I had an on-off relationship for a long time,' she explained, no inflection in her voice. 'We grew up together, went out as teenagers, then broke up when I went away to do my physiotherapy training. I had a couple of casual boyfriends while we were apart and I know Martin dated other people. He stayed in Penhally, apprenticed to his father's construction business, but he was never happy there.' Gabriel waited when she paused again, welcoming the way she twined her fingers with his. 'When I moved back here to work, neither of us were involved with anyone and we started seeing each other again. I suppose we drifted into it for lack of other options. That sounds bad, but we were good friends first and foremost. We just became comfortable with each other, like an old habit. Things were wrong for a long time but neither of us faced up to what was happening.'

'And what did happen?'

'Martin became increasingly restless and withdrawn. He felt stifled by a job he hated, a town he wanted to escape from and a relationship I'm sure he knew deep down was going nowhere. I was settled—I love my job, my friends, my hobbies. But he needed to go off and explore new things and places. And to find someone he could share more than friendship with.'

She sounded understanding and not too sorry that things had ended, Gabriel thought. 'So he left.'

'It was the right decision. We were both relieved.' She smiled, her expression clear. 'A lot of people were shocked—a few had presumed we would marry. That was *never* on the cards. We didn't even live together. It was only once we'd made the final break that I realised how dull and predictable and restricting things had become, and how long it had been since we had been together in any real sense of the word. Our friendship was important but anything more was wrong for us both. Martin needed to leave. We couldn't provide what each other wanted.'

Smiling, she rose to her feet and began to clear the table, moving to the sink to wash up the plates. Thoughtful, understanding the rut she had found herself in, Gabriel drained the last of his wine and crossed the kitchen to join her, working silently by her side for a moment. The atmosphere was thick with the ever-present awareness and desire that rippled between them.

When the last plate had been washed and dried, Gabriel turned her to face him. 'And what did you want, Lauren, that you never got from your relationship?'

Gabriel's smoky, accented voice sent shivers down Lauren's spine. Did she dare admit her secret yearnings? She sensed that with Gabriel she could experience all the things she now knew she had been missing. His compelling gaze drew her in, mesmerised her. The last two weeks had been leading up to this point and they both knew it. Taking her courage in both hands, she looked into his eyes, holding nothing back.

'I wanted things to be more passionate, more spontaneous, less boring.'

'You'd like to be adventurous, *chérie*?'

'Yes,' she whispered, her own voice low and throaty in response to the dark sensuality lacing his.

He didn't move. He wasn't touching her in any way but it

felt as if he was. 'You want to experiment, to be fully satisfied.' It was a statement, not a question, and Lauren swallowed, a shiver of desire skimming down her spine.

'Yes.' The admission was torn from her.

'You want a partner to be your equal, to explore the full scope of your sexuality, to surprise you and challenge you. To give and to take. To break rules and test boundaries.'

Speech was now impossible. He was seducing her with his words, his voice, the promise that remained as yet unspoken. Excitement fired her blood. The wicked glint in his sexy dark eyes made her breathless. She had no doubt that making love with Gabriel would never be boring or predictable or lacking in passion. Her heart pounded beneath her ribs. Unable to wrest her gaze from his, she nodded her answer, aroused beyond bearing, unable to look away from the flare of desire that turned his brown eyes almost black.

He stepped closer, reaching out to take her hands in his. It was their only point of contact and yet her whole body vibrated with sensation. His arms encircled her, his fingers linked with hers so that their joined hands fisted at the small of her back. The movement caused her body to arch and press against his. Every thud of her heart sounded loud in the silence of the kitchen and her breathing sped up, matching the uneven rate of his.

A gasp escaped unchecked as his lips whispered over hers, the tip of his tongue teasing as he circled it round the outline of her mouth, pausing to stroke each corner. It was incredibly erotic. She moaned, opening involuntarily, seeking closer contact, her lips clinging to his as he gave her what she needed. From the first second the kiss flared out of control, deep and demanding as they all but devoured each other, exploring, tongues duelling and entwining. His teeth nibbled at her, inflaming her senses. He pulled on her lips, then sucked on her tongue, drawing her into him. She couldn't get close enough, intoxicated by the male taste of him and his warm, citrusy, masculine scent.

The next moment, she found both her hands restrained behind her by one of his, leaving his other hand free to explore her. And explore her he did. His fingers trailed her face and down her throat, setting little fires wherever he touched, making every particle of her skin tingle. She whimpered when his mouth abandoned hers. Forcing heavy lids to open, her eyes focused to find him watching her, following the path of his fingertips over her flesh. As he bent her back, his palm splayed over her skin, stroking across from one collar-bone to the other before slowly grazing lower. Lauren held her breath as his thumb dipped down her cleavage, tantalisingly brushing against the swell of her breasts, setting her aflame, making her ache for a firmer touch.

'Gabe…'

Her breath rasped out again as his fingers went to work on her buttons, peeling back her top and freeing one breast from the confinement of her lacy red bra. The sight of his darker skin against her paler tones enthralled and excited her. Her nipple, already peaked and flushed with arousal, tightened further under his hungry gaze. She quivered as the pad of his thumb brushed around the outside edge of her areola before gliding once over the proud crest, making her cry out at the sweet ache. After an agonising delay, when she thought she would die of anticipation, his palm cupped the firm fullness of her breast, shaping, testing, before plumping it up as his head lowered. She tried unsuccessfully to free her hands, desperate to touch him, but he kept her captive to his will. Her knees turned to jelly as the moist warmth of his mouth closed over her swollen flesh and he suckled her deeply.

'Oh, my!' She sobbed, shocked by the powerful sensations crashing through her, more intense and incredible than she had ever felt before. Her body arched further in response to his sensual caresses, the rhythmic, hot, heavy pull of his mouth at her breast spearing a devastating ache of need straight to her womb. 'Please. Gabe, please!'

He finally released her hands and she clutched at his shoulders to keep from melting to the floor. Cupping her rear, his fingers flexing, shaping her through the denim as he sank to a chair, he drew her down so she was straddling his lap. Swiftly he dispensed with her shirt and bra. He arched her back, supporting her spine with one hand as the fingers of his other hand traced her skin, learning the contours and textures of her body.

'*Tu es parfait, ma belle,*' he praised huskily, his accent more pronounced. 'Perfect.'

His mouth moved to lavish attention on her neglected breast, bringing the nipple to an aching ripeness to rival its twin. Lauren wriggled on his lap, making him groan as she rubbed herself against the hard thickness of his arousal. She glided one hand up his neck to the back of his head, holding him to her. His close-cropped hair tickled her palm, feeling softly spiky to her touch. Unable to wait any longer to see him, to feel more of him, her fingers tugged at his cable-knit jumper, and he drew back just long enough for her to wrench it over his head. As her fingers traced his upper arms, he returned his avid attention to her breasts, driving her insane with the devastating skill of his hands and mouth, tormenting with his lips and teeth before salving with his tongue. Again he suckled strongly, taking her flesh deep inside, rolling her swollen nipple against the roof of his mouth with his tongue. She cried out, already on the ragged edge, shocked by the urgency of her need.

'I can't bear it!'

He chuckled, the huff of his breath against her over-stimulated flesh nearly sending her past the point of no return. She had never responded to any man the way she did to Gabriel.

He only had to look at her to arouse her. One touch and she was primed, ready. Now she was a whisper away from climaxing and they still had most of their clothes on!

'Hold on, *chérie*.'

Taking her by surprise, he stood up, lifting her with him. She curled her legs around his hips and her arms around his neck, as he headed out of the room towards the stairs. She wanted this with a fierceness that shocked her. They had been heading here since the first moment they had seen each other. Excited anticipation rippled through her. Her hands explored his shoulders and back, delighting in the smoothness of his warm supple skin, the feel of hard muscles rippling beneath.

The rest of the house was in darkness and she pressed her face to his neck, not wanting to acknowledge how little she could see. Instead, she lost herself in his scent, the feel of him, the rightness of her body against his. His hand on her rear tightened, one finger wickedly dipping down to stroke the seam of her jeans over her most sensitive flesh. She moaned, her body reacting instantly, and she wriggled, trying to assuage the terrible ache, desperate for release.

When they reached his bedroom, he set her on her feet, keeping hold of her as he leaned over and switched on the twin bedside lights, casting their welcome glow in the room, easing her anxiety and helping her to see.

He cupped her face with his hands, his expression serious. 'Things in my life are unsettled at the moment, Lauren, and I need to make decisions about my future.'

'Is this about why you left France?' she ventured, nerves tightening her insides.

'Yes. There are family issues.' He hesitated, his uncertainty evident. 'I'm not ready to talk about it. When I am, it will be to you.'

She nodded. 'I understand.' And she did. She wasn't ready to get into her whole family situation either, or face the scary subject of her changing sight. No way would she push him but she would be there if and when he needed her.

'I hadn't planned on or expected to get involved in anything here.'

Terrified he was going to call a halt, she began to protest. 'I—'

'However…' The pad of his thumb pressed gently against her mouth and silenced her. 'I cannot deny the connection that sparked between us from the first moment, or the attraction and longing I have for you. I want you…badly.' Her body tingled, her legs felt weak, and hopeful excitement stirred within her. 'I've not dated at all since my last relationship ended a year ago.'

She was surprised. 'Because you still love her?' she dared to ask.

'No. I didn't love her.' Gabriel smiled and she read the truth in his eyes. 'Like you and Martin, Adèle and I had no grand passion. One day I'll explain, but it ended because of deceit and manipulation. I was angry. It's made me cautious, and I have not been interested in a woman since. Until you.' He paused a moment, then continued. 'I can't make any promises at the moment, Lauren. I—'

'Let's not worry about the future or waste time assessing what this is. I'm not expecting anything or asking for commitment, Gabe, but I don't do one-night stands.'

'Neither do I. I don't embark on things lightly.' His thumbs brushed across her cheekbones. 'I can't give you any guarantees now but this is a hell of a lot more than one night for me. If that's what you want, too.'

'It is.'

Lauren knew the decision had been made the instant she had met him. She meant what she said. She wasn't holding him to anything, but she couldn't deny the hope flaring within her or quell the sense that the chemistry between them was special. She planned to explore it to the fullest and see where this exciting journey took them.

'Why don't we enjoy what we have and see what happens down the line?' she suggested. It had been a long time for her—for him, too, apparently—and she craved Gabriel with an intensity that was almost scary. 'Later will take care of itself.'

'I agree. We live for the here and now.'

She sucked in a breath as his touch became caressing and the flare of sultry desire returned to his eyes. His fingers whispered down her throat, stroking her skin as they trailed between her breasts, neglecting for the moment the flesh that most craved his caresses. Instead, he journeyed down, over and around her navel, making her muscles clench, before grazing down to the waistband of her jeans and working all too slowly to unfasten them.

Lauren was glad he had left the light on. She wanted to see him, to experience everything of their time together. Heat flared inside her as his fingers slid inside the loosened waistband of her jeans, moving down to cuddle her rear. Her own hands settled against his bare chest, enjoying the freedom to touch him. She wanted to linger, to learn every inch of him, but she was too impatient, too needy. She ran her nails lightly over his bronze nipples, smiling at his reaction as he groaned, his body trembling. Moving closer, she set her mouth to him, nipping, licking and teasing, heady from the male taste of him.

Gabriel fisted a hand in her hair, drawing her mouth away from his chest, his eyes dark with a hunger that drove her wild. She sought his kiss, but he denied her, kneeling in front of her to remove her ankle boots and strip off her jeans, revealing the French knickers she favoured, the red lace matching her discarded bra.

'Very nice,' he murmured, nuzzling against her, taking her back to the edge of reason.

Oh, so slowly, he eased the lingerie away. His fingers tormented her, skimming up the backs of her legs, stroking her inner thighs, withholding the touch she most needed. Instead he set his mouth to her navel and used his lips, teeth and tongue to drive her crazy with want.

Just as her legs became too shaky to hold her upright any longer, Gabriel swept her off her feet and tumbled her to the huge four-poster bed that had featured in so many of her dreams in the last two weeks. Dreams that were becoming a reality. She lay there, breathless with expectation, watching hungrily as he kicked off his shoes then took off his faded jeans and black briefs. The breath locked in her lungs as she took in his wonderful physique, the blatant, beautiful male-ness of him, her stomach tightening and her mouth watering as she looked at his impressive erection.

'All right?'

Way more than all right. She nodded at his husky query, involuntarily licking her lips. *'Magnifique,'* she whispered with anticipatory delight.

Smiling, he took an unopened box of condoms from a drawer and put them on the bedside chest after ripping off the outer plastic covering. Then he unsnapped the watch on his right wrist and set it aside. Unable to wait any longer, she held out her hand and he took it, joining her on the bed, drawing her into a deeply intense and arousing kiss. Gabriel rolled them over until she was beneath him and she welcomed the weight of his body on hers. She lost all ability to think as his hands and his mouth laid claim to her body, rapidly taking her to a fever-pitch of need.

'Please,' she demanded, uncaring that she was begging.

'All in good time.'

'Now!'

Gabe chuckled at her plea, sending another stimulating huff of warm air across her taut nipple. 'There's no hurry.'

'There is,' she whimpered, part of her craving release at

once, part of her never wanting the delicious torture to end. 'Gabe, I can't.'

'Trust me, you can…and you will.'

'Wait until it's your turn,' she threatened, making him chuckle again, the throaty, seductive sound tightening everything feminine inside her.

'I'm looking forward to it, *chérie*. Now be still and let me enjoy you.'

No way could she be still! Her body arched and bowed and writhed to his intensely sensual and skilful caresses as he journeyed slowly down to settle between her thighs and use his mouth to take her to paradise. She was the instrument and he was the virtuoso musician and conductor, orchestrating her downfall, playing her to a shattering orgasmic crescendo. Gabriel unleashed a depth of passion and sexuality from within her that she'd had no idea was there. She had enjoyed making love in the past, but she had never experienced this all-consuming, out-of-control explosion of earthy desire and searing need before.

She had barely re-established a tentative grip on reality when he eased two fingers inside her, setting up a rhythmic stroking that threatened to turn the aftershocks still rippling through her into an earthquake of unprecedented proportions. Her heart pounded, her lungs burned, and every nerve ending zinged with sensation. She couldn't bear it. It was incredible, terrible, wonderful. Far too much and yet nowhere near enough. Shaken by her total abandonment, she tried to rein in the litany of cries and moans and whimpers clamouring for escape. She'd never been noisy before. Now, on the point of another explosive climax, she pressed a hand to her mouth to bank down the uncharacteristic scream rising inside her.

'No. Let it go, *ma belle*,' Gabriel demanded huskily against her ear, his tongue teasing her before he sucked on her lobe.

Her hand dropped away as he encouraged her, pushing her to shed any remaining inhibitions. 'Gabe!'

'I want to hear your pleasure.' His fingers intensified their erotic torment, joined by his thumb that circled her clitoris, sending her shooting back into orbit, his rough, accented voice urging her for more. 'That's it. Again. Come for me.'

Gabriel relentlessly took her from peak to impossible peak. Just as she was sure she was totally spent and satisfied, he protected them with a condom, then his hands found hers, their fingers linking, grasping, holding on tightly as he finally united his body with hers. Any remaining breath she had struggled to maintain was stolen as she cried out at the blissful reality of his slow, deep, total penetration.

Lauren couldn't look away from him, trapped by the searing heat in his eyes. She had never felt so taken, so possessed, so complete. Had never shared such intense intimacy—laid bare, as if he could see into her soul. For endless moments he remained still and she savoured his delicious invasion. But she didn't want him to wait. He *had* to move. *Now.* Her hips lifted and rotated in encouragement, demanding a response, and he needed no further invitation. As he slowly withdrew, only to return with more urgency, laying claim to her in a way she had never experienced before, her grip tightened on his hands. His fingers returned the pressure of hers and they anchored each other, swept along on an unstoppable tide.

Lauren surrendered herself totally to Gabriel and the unparalleled joy of making love with him. The friction and pressure were exquisite, the sense of fullness unbelievable. She drew her legs higher, wrapping them around him, taking all of him, drawing him deeper still. He groaned, his control slipping as his movements intensified, harder, heavier, faster.

'Yes, yes.' She sobbed, matching his rhythm, losing all sense of reality as the unimaginable pleasure built wave after wave, threatening to swamp her. 'Please, Gabe. More.'

He gave everything, took everything, demanded everything. She did the same. Together they drove each other higher and further, caught in a raging firestorm of passion that engulfed them and carried them over the edge, consumed by the flames, surrendering to the ecstasy, tumbling into oblivion.

They collapsed together, fighting for breath, their hearts thundering in unison. As Gabriel released her hands and wrapped his arms around her, Lauren clung to him, shaking, shattered, rapturous, scared to let go in case she never found her way back to earth again. An aeon later Gabriel eased his weight from her. She protested, not wanting him to go, but he drew her with him, pulling her even closer and burying his face in her neck. Lauren tightened her hold, inhaling his scent, stunned by the incredible experience they had shared.

'*Mon Dieu.*' Gabriel's voice was throaty and raw. He sounded as overwhelmed as she felt. Slumberous dark eyes looked into hers, his fingers shaking as he brushed damp tendrils of hair back from her cheek. 'Are you all right?'

Lauren licked lips still plump and tingly from his deliciously erotic kisses. 'I don't know. You?'

'Not sure.'

'That was…' Still dazed, she searched for the right word. 'It was…'

'Wow,' Gabriel volunteered huskily, cradling her against him.

That pretty much covered it in any language, Lauren decided. 'Exactly.'

She was never going to get enough of this man. He did things to her she had never imagined, made her feel things she had never thought possible and took her to places she had never been before. She had no idea what the future held in store for them beyond his stay in Penhally, but she wanted Gabriel to be part of her days…and her nights…for as long as possible.

CHAPTER SIX

THE weeks leading up to Christmas sped by and Gabriel had never felt so content…settled both at work and in his private life. Being with Lauren was the most amazing thing that had ever happened to him. A smile curved his mouth just thinking about her. The first patient for his Saturday morning surgery having cancelled, he had a few moments before the next person arrived, so he leaned back in his chair, his hands linked behind his head, and thought back to that first night he and Lauren had spent together.

He had known from the moment that they had met that there was an inexplicable and special connection between them, one that transcended the undeniable physical attraction. The first time they had made love had proved him right. He'd never experienced anything like it before. Incredibly, it had just got better and better since…not only in the intensity of their passion but in the deepening of their close bond and instinctive trust. In bed they matched each other in adventurousness, pushing each other to explore the boundaries of their desire and sensuality. Their rapport and innate friendship meant they were perfect companions personally and fully supportive and complementary colleagues professionally.

The only subjects that remained taboo were their family histories—his in particular—and Lauren's sight. A frown creased his brow. After lingeringly making love a second time that first night, they had fallen into an exhausted sleep, only for him to wake in the early hours when Lauren had slipped out of bed. Unknown to her, he had watched as she had tried to find her way to the bathroom through the unfamiliar room, one hand extended out in front of her, feeling her way in the dark, taking cautious, baby steps, bumping into things. He'd waited until she had been in the *en suite* before switching the bedside lamps back on, noting the way she hesitated when she came out, looking uncertain. Not wanting to spoil things or to confront her about the issues with her vision, he had smiled and pulled back the duvet.

'I missed you, *chérie*.'

More sure of her footing with the lamps casting a glow in the room, she had hurried back to bed and he had given himself up to the blissful magic of her mouth and her hands on his body. But the incident had convinced him that Lauren was exhibiting night blindness. There had been several more moments over the weeks, little things he had noticed but which Lauren had brushed aside, and he had not found the right moment to talk to her about it. In truth he was scared of saying or doing anything to spoil what they had, so he kept putting it off, telling himself he would wait until something happened that could not be ignored. But Lauren's problem nagged at him. Had she always been lost in the dark? Was there some simple cause? Or was her night blindness a symptom of something more serious?

His fears had been compounded following a conversation with Chloe last week. Worried about Diane Bailey, one of her mums-to-be, Chloe had asked for a doctor to accompany her to the woman's home and, with Oliver unavailable, Gabriel had been happy to help. Having had a terrible time delivering her first baby, the young mother had been understandably terrified at facing the birth of her second child. She was determined to have a home birth, refusing to go to St Piran's for the delivery in case she suffered as she had at another hospital whose overstretched staff had failed to give her proper care and consideration. Between them, he and Chloe—the best midwife he had ever worked with—had allayed many of the woman's fears and promised to work together as a team to give her the safest birth possible and ensuring her their constant support.

On the way back to the surgery Chloe had surprised him by pulling over to the side of the road. 'Gabriel, can I talk to you for a moment?'

'Yes, of course.' Concerned, he'd turned to study her. 'Is something wrong?'

'Lauren saved my life,' she had told him softly after a long pause.

Gabriel had listened in horror as Chloe confided in him about her past with her abusive father, her green eyes shadowed with remembered pain as she had told him of the last beating and how Lauren had rescued her and helped her escape. '*Mon Dieu*, Chloe. I am so sorry. I had no idea.'

'No one but Lauren and Oliver know the full story. And now you.'

'Your secret is safe with me,' he'd assured her.

'She saved my life back then…now Oliver is teaching me to live it to the fullest. I'd do anything for her.' She paused a moment, nibbling her lower lip in indecision. 'Gabriel, have you noticed anything, I don't know…*off*…about Lauren?'

He felt his own guard slipping into place. 'What do you mean?'

'I'm probably being silly.'

'Go on,' he encouraged when she hesitated.

'Everybody has always teased Lauren because of her clumsiness, her habit of doing daft things and having minor accidents. She has terrible hand-eye co-ordination.' Anxiety and confusion had replaced her earlier indecision. 'The incidents seem to be happening more often these days. When Oliver first came here in June, he didn't know of Lauren's reputation for mishaps and I had the feeling he believed there was more to what was happening than her just being clumsy. He wouldn't say more and I'm scared to bring the subject up again. It's just...' Again Chloe paused, her worry for her friend evident.

'Just what? Tell me.'

'I don't know how to explain.' Sighing, she shook her head. 'Spending more time with Lauren at Gatehouse Cottage because of the flood damage to my place in Fisherman's Row, I've noticed little things I'd never been aware of before. Odd things. And then there's her painting. She's so talented and she loves her art. In the summer I bought a picture for Oliver's birthday present and was looking around her studio—it was the first time I'd been there in a while. I noticed subtle differences in her newer works, less detail, more fuzziness, but Lauren denied it. Shortly after that she stopped painting altogether. I tried to ask her about it and she got defensive, made excuses.'

She looked away from him for a moment and took a deep breath before rushing on. 'Plus she seems reluctant to go out at night. Not that we've had many opportunities lately with the other girls in our circle of friends busy with new babies and husbands, Vicky away and myself being with Oliver. But Lauren doesn't even seem keen on going to the cinema now.'

'Is that new? Has she been confident in the dark until recently?' he probed, concerned that Lauren's lack of night vision was not a long-standing issue after all.

'I've never noticed that nervousness in the dark before. It's like the way she used the chance to change her work hours so she does her home visits in the mornings. I sense something is wrong, Gabriel, but I don't know what to do. I'm so delighted you and Lauren are together...' she flashed him a sweet smile '…but I wondered if you saw whatever Oliver did, what the rest of us who have known her for years have missed because it's always been there or worsened slowly.'

'Chloe, I—' He broke off, unsure what to say.

She rested a hand on his arm. 'I don't want to put you in a difficult position. But I care about Lauren and I *am* worried. Can I just ask that if you have any doubts or concerns in future, you'll talk to Oliver to see if you both think the same and if there is anything you can do to help her?'

'I can promise you that, Chloe, yes.'

He would keep the promise he had made but not yet. Not until something more specific happened that gave him real evidence of a problem. Part of him was relieved to know he was not alone in noticing the odd, erratic and worrying things about Lauren's poor night vision. But the rest of him was wary of invading her privacy, unsure how to get Lauren to talk about something she had so clearly not even acknowledged for herself. He *would* talk to Oliver—if and when the time came that he had to intervene.

In the meantime, scared about Lauren driving at night— even though the only time she took the car out after dark was for the short drive home from the surgery—he had managed to contrive a new routine. They now went home together, leaving her car at work where it was ready for her morning house calls. He wasn't sure how long he could get away with it without arousing Lauren's suspicions.

Since their first night together Lauren had virtually moved into the Manor House with him, leaving Oliver and Chloe at Gatehouse Cottage, although they got together often for meals and the occasional trip out when they were all off duty at the same time. At work he and Lauren were totally professional, keeping their private life separate from the surgery, but their relationship had never been a secret. Without exception, everyone had accepted them as a couple and were happy for them, especially Oliver, Chloe and Kate. Even Hazel had warmed to him.

As the days and weeks went by, they had enjoyed time alone as well as taking part in community events. They had been to the local firework display on Guy Fawkes night, eating toffee-apples and cuddling up in front of the bonfire to keep warm. They had explored the local environment, walking with Foxy who was growing more confident all the time. They had jogged, listened to music, spent time with Oliver and Chloe, and had talked for hours about everything and anything but their taboo subjects. Most of all, they had made love…everywhere, every way and as frequently as possible. A smile replaced his frown. By rights he should be worn out! But he was energised, happier than he ever remembered being. Any doubts and worries about what was going to happen when his time in Penhally was over, he forcibly set from his mind.

The ringing of the telephone brought an end to his reverie and he leaned forward, reaching for the receiver. 'Yes, Sue?' he asked of the head receptionist.

'Adrian Westcott is here, Gabriel,' the friendly, efficient woman informed him. 'He's a few minutes early but I thought you would like to know—it isn't every day we're ahead of schedule.'

Gabriel chuckled. 'Indeed not. Thanks, Sue. Please, send him through.'

After hanging up, he pulled the notes out of the tray and had a quick glance at them before rising to greet his patient. In his early forties, with thinning blond hair and pale blue eyes, the man looked tired and dejected.

'Hello, Adrian,' he said, shaking the man's hand. 'Please, take a seat.' He waited a moment as Adrian made himself comfortable. 'What can I do for you today?'

'It's about my tinnitus, Doctor. It's worsening all the time, as is my hearing, and affecting my work. Things are really getting me down.'

'What work do you do?'

'I'm a teacher at the secondary school.' Adrian grimaced and shook his head. 'I love my job but it's harder to cope with the noise levels or several people talking at once, not to mention making sure I'm hearing my students properly.'

Gabriel glanced again at the notes to see what history and previous advice had been recorded. 'You saw a specialist ten years ago and you were told you had otosclerosis?'

'That's right. I lived in the north of England then. I moved here for the job with my family eight years ago. No one really explained what it meant to have otosclerosis, just that I had to live with the tinnitus, that there was nothing much to be done.'

'Tinnitus is a symptom that has many causes and is experienced in different ways. For most types there isn't a cure. Otosclerosis means that the bones in the middle ear harden and this affects the hearing as it prevents the bones vibrating. It can lead to deafness. What kind of noises do you hear with your tinnitus?' he asked, making notes as his patient explained.

'It's a whooshing noise but throbs and thumps like my pulse, as if I'm hearing my heartbeat all the time. I've had it for fifteen years or more. For a while I tried to follow the advice to cover up the sounds, but it's progressively got worse, to the point I can't ignore it. And my hearing is diminishing.' Adrian paused, a deep sigh escaping. 'One on one with people I'm not too bad, I'm learning to lipread, but in a gathering or with other noises, it's becoming impossible. My wife encouraged me to come, to try again, even though I doubt there is much you can do.'

Gabriel considered the options, feeling for the man and his situation. 'What you describe is pulsatile tinnitus. It's many years since you saw the specialist and things may have changed since then, so I'd like to refer you to a consultant at the audiology department at St Piran's. He'll do a thorough reassessment.' He paused a moment, not wanting to give any false hope. 'There is an operation that works for some sufferers of otosclerosis that involves removing the stapes and replacing it with an artificial plastic bone. It's high risk and carries a chance of deafness during the operation, but if successful it gives improved hearing and a reduction in the tinnitus. They do the worst ear first. But all this is dependent on what the surgeon has to say when he sees you—and on what risk you want to take.'

'I certainly want to find out about it,' Adrian enthused, looking much happier than he had when he'd arrived.

'I can't promise that you will qualify, or that it would work.'

The man nodded at the warning. 'I understand. But it's worth exploring…better than doing nothing and just going on as I am. You live with something for so long and the changes creep up on you slowly, so you learn to live with it. Often it's only when something unusual or big happens that you realise just how bad things have become and how much you have deteriorated,' he added and Gabriel frowned, thinking of Lauren and what could be a similar pattern with her sight.

'I'll write to the consultant and arrange for him to see you,' Gabriel reassured him, focusing back on his patient. 'I'm not sure what the waiting time is but we'll get things moving as quickly as we can in the new year.'

As Gabriel rose to show Adrian out a few moments later, the man turned at the door and shook his hand. 'Whatever happens, I can't tell you what a difference it makes to have someone understand and take me seriously. Thank you so much, Dr Devereux.'

'No problem. Call me any time if you need anything explained or have any problems.'

His appointments continued smoothly for the rest of the morning and, after tackling some of the mountain of paperwork, he was able to leave and meet up with Oliver for a pub lunch. Lauren had gone out with Chloe for the day to do some last-minute Christmas shopping. He couldn't wait for her to come home.

It was the last weekend before Christmas and the shops in Newquay had been manic. Thankful to escape the crowds, Lauren wedged her purchases with Chloe's in the back of her friend's car before sinking thankfully into the passenger seat.

'Oh, boy, my feet are killing me.'

'Tell me about it.' Chloe slid behind the wheel and sighed. 'I can't believe we got everything done.'

'I don't want to see another shop or hear another tinny carol ever again.'

Chloe chuckled, steering the car out of the parking zone and heading out of town towards home. 'You'll get a second wind. Let's hope Oliver and Gabriel have managed to pick out decent trees. Do you think we were right to entrust the job to them?'

'They'll be fine.' Lauren wasn't so fussed about all the Christmas paraphernalia as Chloe but she kept her thoughts to herself, knowing how miserable Chloe's childhood had been and how much she wanted this first Christmas with Oliver to be perfect. 'That set of baby clothes you got for Rachel Kenner's little boy are so cute.'

'Thanks. I can't wait to see him. I'm just so relieved both she and the baby are well after the birth. Rachel's naming the baby Daniel after her father,' Chloe added, a wobble in her voice.

Lauren smiled in sympathy. 'She's been through so much, the poor girl, but she's remarkable, the way she's handled everything.'

'She is. And her aunt and uncle have been wonderfully supportive.'

Dusk was falling as they arrived back at Gatehouse Cottage and Lauren wasted no time in switching on plenty of lights as soon as she went inside. Foxy greeted her enthusiastically. After she and Chloe had unloaded the car and hidden away their packages, they sank down for a reviving cup of tea while they waited for Gabriel and Oliver to come back. Foxy laid his head on her knee and she stroked him.

'Lauren?'

'Hmm?'

'I want to tell you something.'

Alerted by the uncertainty mixed with excitement in her friend's voice, Lauren opened her eyes and looked over at Chloe. 'Is anything wrong?'

'Nothing, it's just…' A blush pinkened Chloe's cheeks.

'You're pregnant!'

'No! No, that's not it.'

'Sorry.' She sent Chloe a rueful smile. 'Everyone in Penhally seems to have been breeding like rabbits this year! I wouldn't have been surprised.'

'I know! And I do want children one day. We both do. For now all this is so new to me and I just want time to be alone with Oliver, to enjoy being a couple,' she explained, her blush deepening.

Lauren fought a grin. 'Of course you do.' Chloe was such a sweetheart and it was obvious that she was more than well loved—and satisfied—thanks to Oliver. As she deserved to be.

'The thing is…' Chloe's green eyes sparkled with delight. 'This is a secret and you can't tell anyone. Except Gabriel.'

'OK, I promise,' she agreed, reaching for her tea.

'Oliver and I are eloping.'

'What?' Lauren nearly dropped her mug she was so surprised at Chloe's rushed announcement. Setting it safely on the table, she faced her friend. She felt Foxy's tension at her sudden movements and soothed him. 'You're eloping? When?'

Chloe positively bounced with excitement. 'Over Christmas. But we don't want to spoil anything for you.' Worry momentarily dulled the gleam in her eyes. 'Gabriel isn't going back to France for the holiday, is he?'

'I don't know. We've not discussed it,' Lauren admitted with a frown.

'Well, I know it's an awful cheek, but Oliver's asking Gabriel today if he'd mind covering for him. Kate knows I'm taking my remaining week's holiday, but not why. We're hoping not to have to tell Nick. You know he can be a bit starchy about things.'

'He does have set ideas,' Lauren agreed. 'It's so exciting, but why all the cloak-and-dagger stuff?'

It was Chloe's turn to frown. 'We're getting a lot of interference from Oliver's family. It's well meant,' she hastened to explain, 'but neither Oliver nor I want some huge fuss and production made of it. And with Reverend Kenner gone and no permanent replacement here in Penhally, I'd feel weird getting married in the local church,' she finished, and Lauren felt a shiver of empathy.

'I can understand that. So what's the plan? Can you tell me?'

'Oliver has a friend he trained with in London who has a glorious cottage in southern Scotland. He's loaning it to us. We found out all about it three months ago and got the necessary permissions. We've sent the papers back to the registrar and we're getting married at Gretna in the traditional Old Blacksmith's Shop! We'll be back the day after New Year,' she confided, bubbling over with happiness.

Chloe's enthusiasm was infectious and Lauren was thrilled for her. 'How romantic!'

'I can't wait! I hope everyone will understand. We plan to have a party for all our friends later in January.'

'Do what's right for you and don't worry about anyone else,' Lauren urged, reaching out to take her hand. 'You know I'll support you. I just want you to be happy—and I know Oliver is the man for you. It's wonderful seeing you together.'

Tears shimmered in Chloe's eyes. 'Thanks.'

As they talked more about the secret wedding plans it was impossible not to share Chloe's excitement. Although nothing had been said about Christmas and New Year, Lauren was certain Gabriel would do all he could to cover for Oliver. She'd miss her friends over the holiday, but the thought of being alone with Gabriel held its own appeal. The man was amazing! His dimpled smile pulled at something inside her. And she could listen to him for ever. That softly husky voice with the delicious accent always made her stomach turn over and sent a tingle of awareness down her spine.

The bond had formed quickly between them. Friendship, respect and trust mingled with instant attraction and high-octane passion deepening and swelling her swiftly growing feelings for him. She tried to live every moment, as they had agreed, and not think about what was going to happen in the future, but it was impossible to imagine not having Gabriel in her life.

He was a wonderfully inventive lover, exciting, erotic, wicked, challenging her to really let go and experiment. She had never experienced such pleasure, such closeness, such utter bliss as she did with him. He brought all her secret fantasies to life. The desire and passion between them seemed to increase, not diminish, blazing ever hotter with every passing day.

The only black moments came as she tried to cover up her increasingly scary sight problems. The night blindness was now a major and permanent problem. She was pretty sure that Gabriel had noticed her difficulties, her clumsy moments when her sight failed her, but he'd not brought the subject up and she was grateful. Equally grateful that they had fallen into going home together most nights so she didn't have to drive. She suspected Gabriel was doing it on purpose but she was too thankful to make an issue of it.

That Chloe and Oliver were aware of some changes was obvious. Several times Chloe had mentioned painting and Lauren hadn't been able to explain why she had stopped the thing she had loved so much for so long. In the summer Chloe had noticed changes in the new paintings, changes Lauren herself didn't want to face up to. When her sight problems had been confined to the dark, she had been able to pretend it didn't matter, but in the last weeks she had noticed that it took longer for her eyes to adjust to changing light, and it was starting to become difficult to distinguish contrasts, even in daylight or under bright light indoors. In the last few days she'd had odd moments when she'd thought her peripheral vision wasn't as sharp as usual. She was frightened, unsure what to do.

'You are the only one, apart from Oliver, I can confide in like this,' Chloe said, and Lauren tried to push her own worries aside. Her friend paused a moment, nibbling her lower lip, the expression in her green eyes serious. 'You know you can always talk to me about anything, too, don't you, Lauren?'

She forced a smile and kept her voice steady, unable to speak aloud the fears that grew more troublesome as the weeks went by. 'Sure.' How much longer could she pretend that nothing was wrong?

Thankfully, Gabriel and Oliver arrived back then, a blast of wintry air sweeping through the cottage as they propped the door open to wrestle a huge, sweetly scented pine tree into the cosy living room. Diverted from her questions, Chloe jumped to her feet, hovering eagerly as the tree, already potted, was positioned, then she threw herself into Oliver's arms.

'Hi, babe,' he welcomed her, enfolding her in a hug. Lauren saw him glance at Gabriel before he looked at her. 'Have you told Lauren?'

Beaming, Chloe nodded. 'Yes.'

'Gabriel's happy to help out and he's going to cover my

shifts for me the week we're away—and look after Pirate and Cyclops,' Oliver informed his bride-to-be, laughing as she rushed to hug Gabriel, too.

'Thank you so much!'

'My pleasure, Chloe,' Gabriel reassured her.

Lauren stroked Foxy before she, too, rose to her feet. 'Congratulations, Oliver.' Smiling, she kissed his cheek. 'I'm so happy for you both,' she added, hugging Chloe.

After enjoying a celebratory glass of wine, Lauren happily agreed when Gabriel suggested they return to the Manor House. 'I'm sure you and Chloe would like some time alone and I still have another Christmas tree to wrestle with,' he joked.

'Do you want me to come and help?' Oliver offered, walking with them towards the front door, Foxy trotting ahead.

'We'll be fine.'

It felt odd, standing in the small hallway of her own house, leaving her friends there, as if she were the visitor, and going back with Gabriel to the Manor House where she felt so right and content. She was about to step outside, grateful the lights were illuminating the short pathway, when Oliver stopped her.

'Sorry, Lauren, I forgot. There's a pile of mail for you,' he told her, handing her a stack of envelopes held together by an elastic band.

'Thanks.'

Once at the Manor House, Lauren switched on the lights downstairs and settled Foxy in the kitchen with his food while Gabriel managed to manoeuvre a beautifully shaped tree that smelled as delicious as the one Oliver had bought, into the living room. Lauren joined him. While she may not be as excited about the festivities as Chloe, she was looking forward to decorating the tree with Gabriel and to them spending time together. She thought of the presents she had bought him, now hidden safely away until she had some time alone to wrap

them, and hoped he would like them, that she had found the
right balance and hadn't gone too over the top.

'I didn't see the elopement coming.' Kneeling on the floor
to light the log fire, Gabriel chuckled. 'Did you?'

Lauren sat on the sofa, the pile of unopened mail in her lap.
'No. But I'm not surprised. In fact, I'm delighted for them,
they're so perfect together.'

'Indeed.'

'You're sure you are OK with taking on the extra shifts?
You weren't planning to go back to France for the holiday?'
she probed cautiously.

'Hell, no.' Gabriel paused, glancing over his shoulder. 'I
know I've been close-mouthed about it, but I'm not in any
hurry to go home.'

Unsure of the issues but having every faith that he not only
had his reasons but had done nothing wrong, she placed a
hand on his shoulder. 'It's OK. I'm certainly not complain-
ing about having the chance to spend the holiday with you—
even if we are working for part of it.'

'There's no one I want to spend Christmas with but you,
chérie.'

The husky words warmed her right through. Smiling, Lauren
watched for a moment as Gabriel turned back to tend to the fire,
putting some larger logs on as the kindling took hold. She
turned her attention to the mail and sorted through the mixture
of bills, letters and cards, including an oversized postcard of
Cologne cathedral from Vicky, full of excited news and typical
Vicky-isms. Her smile faded, to be replaced by a knot of tension
in her stomach when she recognised the Australian stamps and
familiar handwriting on an air-mail envelope. For a moment she
sat and stared at it then, fingers shaking, she forced herself to
open it. A stupid threat of tears pricked her eyes as she looked
at the plain card. There was no accompanying letter and nothing
written on the inside but two names.

'I know we've avoided talking about our families, Lauren, mine in particular,' Gabriel said, but she barely heard him, focused as she was on the card. 'Lauren?' She jumped when Gabriel's hand settled on her knee and looked up, finding him watching her with concern. 'What is wrong, *ma belle*?'

'You said we avoided families—perhaps that's because family often isn't all it's cracked up to be,' she whispered, sucking in a breath and handing him the card.

Gabriel opened it, then glanced at her with a frown. 'Who are John and Betty?'

'The people I called Mum and Dad for the first twenty-five years of my life.' She managed to say the words without betraying the emotion roiling within her. 'They became John and Betty the moment they told me I was adopted and the pretence of being my parents ended.'

Gabriel cursed, taking one of her hands in his. 'You had no idea until five years ago?'

'No. Don't get me wrong, they were always kind to me. I had everything I needed in terms of a safe and secure home, guidance, the freedom to go my own way…'

'But not the love and cherishing,' he suggested when her words trailed off.

She sighed and ran the fingers of her free hand through her hair. 'I never felt as if I belonged. Like a cuckoo in the nest, I didn't fit. I still don't understand why they waited so long to tell me. Worse was the realisation that had they known they could have their own children after all, they would never have adopted me. I was always second best. Clive was born after I had been with them for two years and they couldn't exactly give me back.'

Gabriel swore again, his fingers linking with hers. 'That's horrible. It must have been a huge shock and very confusing.'

'Yes.' She'd been so unsettled, so angry and hurt when the truth had come out. Yet it had explained so many things. 'I was three months old when they adopted me as a last resort, believing Betty couldn't conceive. It was a big surprise to them when she fell pregnant. They doted on Clive. He was terribly spoiled. We never got on. He knew he was the favourite, the golden boy who could do no wrong. I envied him his special place in their lives, unable to understand what was wrong with me. I think I sensed even at a young age that I was less somehow.'

'Lauren—'

'No, really. All Clive's needs came first. Everything was geared to him and his success. He went off to Australia seven years ago and settled there, marrying a local girl and starting a family. Two years later, wanting to be near their grandchildren, my parents—' she stumbled over the words '—decided to take early retirement and emigrate. Before they left, they told me the whole story, explained their need to go and gave me Gatehouse Cottage as a gift, a pay-off to salve their consciences and feel they had done right by me, I guess.'

A part of her, a part of that child she had once been, craved to be loved for herself…to be really wanted. But she didn't say that aloud. 'Fortunately, I'm happy here—I love my friends and my job.'

'So they just cut you loose? They left you alone to deal with the shock, having told you the truth about your life?' Gabriel protested, his anger on her behalf clear.

'Yes.'

He shook his head and huffed out a breath. 'Do you know anything about your birth parents?'

'Only that they died in an accident shortly after I was born. There weren't any grandparents or siblings to take me in…' not who wanted her, anyway, she added silently '…so I was taken into care and put up for adoption.'

Gabriel didn't say anything for a few moments but Lauren hardly noticed as she was lost in thought. There was so much she wanted to know about the family she had originally come from, not least details of her medical history. Was there any clue among her birth relatives that could explain the weird things happening with her eyesight?

'I understand how disruptive and unsettling learning the truth about your identity can be, Lauren.'

Startled from her reverie, she looked up and saw that the pain in Gabriel's eyes matched that lacing his voice. 'You, too?'

'Yes.'

Hurting for him, she returned the pressure of his fingers. 'Can you tell me now?'

The only sound in the room was the crackling of the flames as they ate into the wood in the fireplace. Lauren held her breath. Was the time right for Gabriel to open up and trust her with the demons that had driven him from his home?

CHAPTER SEVEN

'YOU are not alone in learning late on that everything you thought you knew about yourself, your family, your life is a lie, Lauren. Or in wondering where you fit in.'

As he spoke the words, Gabriel found it easier than he had imagined to confide in Lauren. He had been so contented these last weeks in Penhally Bay that he had largely succeeded in pushing France and the unresolved issues there from his mind. The approach of Christmas had brought them to the fore again. At least this year promised to be more settled and happier. Last year had been the first Christmas without his father, bringing back the pain of his loss and the anger and uncertainty at the secrets that had come to light after his death, leading to a widening of the rift with Yvette and the row about his future.

Lauren had shared her background with him and he more than understood how shocked and hurt she must have felt, learning about her adoption in such a way and then being cut off by the couple who had raised her. The strength of his desire to have been here to support and protect her through such a difficult time took him by surprise and made him realise just how involved his feelings for her had become. He knew with utter conviction that he trusted Lauren completely. Without giving himself any more time to consider his actions, he sat back on his heels in front of the fire and told her things he had never shared with anyone else, laying bare the skeletons in the Devereux family cupboard.

'My father, Pierre, died twenty months ago. He was fifty-eight. It was sudden and unexpected…a big shock. We were very close,' he explained, shying away from the knowledge that his father had kept such an important truth from him. 'I was working at a practice in Paris at the time, in an area that served a poor community and a large immigrant population.'

Lauren edged closer and he was happy to let her take his hand in hers to return the understanding and comfort he had tried to offer her a short while ago. 'Gabe, I'm so sorry about your father.'

'Thank you. The trouble began shortly afterwards.'

'Trouble?' Lauren queried with a frown.

'The exposing of family secrets and lies.' He stared into the flickering flames of the fire and sighed. 'I have always had a difficult relationship with Maman. She was cold, unforgiving, dictatorial, and mostly I was raised by a nanny. I spent a lot of time with Papa, but never with Maman. Now I know why. And why my skin is darker than most of the other members of the family. Yvette Devereux is *not* my mother. She did not give birth to me and she resented it that she had to raise me.'

'Oh, Gabe… How could she?'

He shot Lauren a quick glance but saw nothing but concern and understanding in her slate-grey eyes. 'I only have her side of the story—a story she took vicious delight in telling me after the funeral. Part of me feels betrayed that my father never explained to me himself but, despite that, I did know him and love him and the things Yvette said just don't make sense. I have the feeling she has embellished the truth at best and lied at worst to serve her own ends.'

'What was her explanation?' Lauren asked, encouraging him to talk it out.

'She said that my father had an affair with a lowly woman from Martinique, a *servant*—it infuriated me the way she used that word. He took me away from this woman and demanded Yvette bring me up as her own, using her obsessive sense of duty and fear of sullying the family name to force her to agree. Now she expects me to pay her back for all the years she had to be humiliated and put up with me.'

'That's absurd,' Lauren exploded, gripping his hand. 'You are not to blame for anything. Whatever the truth of your birth, your father—who must have been very young at the time—took you, loved you and raised you. Yvette had choices of her own. Choices that are not your responsibility. What does she expect you to do?'

'The first demand is that I stop playing at being a doctor and—'

'Playing?' she interrupted with outrage.

'To Yvette my career and lifestyle are not good enough for the family name and she sees it as my duty to take my father's place in the running of the family estates, safeguarding her position. She doesn't feel secure that the decisions and the control of finances are left in the hands of my uncle's side of the family, despite the provisions made for her in my father's will.' His cynicism deepened as he thought of Yvette's other plans for him. 'She also expects me to marry someone socially acceptable of her choosing.'

Lauren stared at him, wide-eyed. 'No way. That's archaic and ridiculous.'

'Exactly. But so determined was she that she sent Adèle to Paris to lure me.'

'Lure you?'

'Yes. We went out for a while, but then I found out about the deceit, that Yvette had set me up and was using Adèle to try to ensure I gave up medicine and returned home, especially that I left what Yvette considered an unacceptable job. She made a lot of trouble for me at the practice. Adèle was to be handsomely rewarded with my name…plus the family money and standing, of course, which interested her far more than I did.' He sighed before continuing. 'That's why I needed the space away. First in St Ouen-sur-Mer and now here in Penhally Bay. No matter what levels of guilt my mother tries to lay on me, I have no intention of marrying for convenience.'

'Nor should you. And you can't give up medicine either. It's your *life*.' Lauren squeezed his hand, her gaze earnest. 'You are an amazing doctor, Gabe. You have to live your own life in whatever way is right for you. Don't let Yvette's schemes and any misplaced guilt force you into something that would make you unhappy and change the person you are.'

It felt amazing to have someone believe in him. Cupping her face, he kissed her before drawing her close and wrapping his arms around her. 'Thank you. I think Yvette is bitter that she could never have children of her own and give my father a legitimate heir. Not that I believe theirs was ever a love match—she was as distant to my father as she was to me. She's an attractive woman in a polished, icy kind of way. Everything was, and remains, about duty and appearances to her.' He slid Lauren off the sofa and nestled her more snugly into his embrace, breathing in her scent. 'What hurts is that Papa never explained any of this. I don't know his side of it, what is the whole truth and what is exaggerated. He wasn't a man to avoid anything, no matter how awkward, which makes me more confused that he kept it from me. I thought he approved of my career, that he was proud of me.'

'Of course he was proud of you,' she protested heatedly. 'How could he not be?'

Lauren's loyal support and fierce protectiveness eased some of the tension inside him and he found it easier to continue his story. 'My father and his brother inherited a big estate that includes a vineyard, a farm and assorted business holdings, all funded by my ancestors who made their fortunes in the Caribbean. I find it hard to come to terms with that part of my family history. I feel ashamed that my family's money and success was built on the disenfranchisement and misery of others, even if it was generations ago. I had so many privileges and took them for granted, not knowing it was based on the hard work and sacrifices of those who'd had nothing, often not even their freedom,' he told her, his emotions scarcely held in check.

'You are not accountable for the actions others took years ago. Many businesses and families today are founded on regrettable things from times past. What matters is how *you* act and what you do with those things in your own control.'

'Logically I know that, but…' He hesitated, brushing his free hand over his face. 'It's just been a confusing time with much to try to come to terms with. The identity of my birth mother explains my darker skin—something I share with a couple of distant cousins, which was explained away by the past involvements and dalliances of my great-grandfather and grandfather in the Caribbean. Nothing was said about my father. I want to learn more about my true heritage and find out more about my real mother, but I don't even know her name.'

Lauren's arms tightened around him. 'So many things go through your mind, so many questions that have no answers.'

'Yes.' He stroked her hair, knowing from what she had told him of her own adoption and family circumstances that she understood the sense of rootlessness and uncertainty. 'I never questioned my ethnicity and very identity before. Now…'

An aching vulnerability laced Gabriel's voice, cutting Lauren deep inside. She felt his pain and confusion, knew exactly where he was coming from, and wished she could do more to reassure him and help him find a solution, a *resolution*, to his past. She'd had five years to get her head around who she was and how her perceptions had changed. Gabriel had known for less than two years. And she had not suffered a bereavement. He had lost the father he had loved and who he now questioned. That had to be impossibly hard. If there were things she needed to know, she could ask—it wouldn't be pleasant, but she had the choice. Gabriel didn't. She wished she could ease his heartache, make things right for him, but all she could do was be there to listen and comfort and understand.

As well as mourning his father and dealing with the revelations about his true birth mother, Gabriel still had Yvette to contend with. The woman sounded awful. It was bad enough that she had been emotionally cold to a child in her care, worse that she wanted to change Gabriel and tie him to something so wrong for him. But to insinuate a woman into his life, one who cared nothing for him, with the purpose of influencing him, lying to him, deceiving him was unforgivable. No wonder Gabriel was loath to return to France or have contact with Yvette.

'Never before has the colour of my skin been an issue.'

Startled from her thoughts and shocked by Gabriel's words, Lauren frowned, pulling back to look at him, seeing the shadows dulling his eyes. 'What do you mean?'

'I never questioned my ancestry. If anyone mentioned my skin colour, it didn't bother me. Now comments about it make me feel uncomfortable.'

'Why would anyone mention it? No one in Penhally has said anything, have they?' she asked, unable to imagine anyone being so narrow-minded.

'One or two. Not in a prejudicial way,' he added, and Lauren tamped down her anger on his behalf. 'But I'm conscious of being different…the cuckoo in *my* family, to follow your analogy. That's probably because of the derisive way Yvette spoke of my birth mother, as if the woman was beneath contempt, as if I was worth nothing.'

'Your father didn't think so. He cared about your mother and he loved you.'

'I think so. I hope so. I wish I knew the circumstances, how Papa really felt, if he *did* have feelings for my mother or if I was a mistake,' he murmured.

'I understand the need to uncover your missing roots, to find answers to your questions, but *you* are the same person you've always been.'

As Gabriel released her and moved to put another couple of logs on the fire, Lauren's heart cried out for the uncertainty he was feeling. She studied his handsome profile, the leanly sculpted body outlined under his shirt by the flickering flames, the play of muscle along hair-dusted forearms.

'What?' he asked, a quizzical smile on his face as he turned back to her.

She shook her head, raising a hand to cup his jaw. The end-of-the-day stubble there prickled against her palm, reminding her how exciting and arousing the rasp of it felt on her body as he caressed and explored her with his mouth. Realising he was waiting for her answer, she returned her gaze to his.

'The colour of your skin is not what I see when I look at you.'

'What *do* you see, Lauren?' he asked huskily, taking her hand and moving it so he could kiss her palm, his tongue tracing teasing circles, igniting the fiery need for him that always simmered inside her.

'I see *you*. All that makes you the man you are. An excellent doctor…one who shows great care and consideration for his patients, and…'

He nibbled on her fingers, momentarily stealing her breath and her words as he slowly sucked each one in turn into his mouth, distracting her. 'And?'

'And,' she continued, trying to force the words past the constriction in her throat, every part of her trembling with desire, 'I see a gorgeous man who is warm and intelligent, funny and generous. A man who is great to be with, who is a loyal friend, who makes me feel good…and who is incredibly sexy.' Her breath ragged, her voice rough with emotion, she looked deep into his eyes, seeing how they darkened with answering passion. 'Gabe, you are beautiful just as you are.'

She gasped in surprise as he caught her to him, one hand threading through her hair to hold her still for his inflaming, hungry kiss. Kneeling in front of him, she opened her mouth hotly in welcome. His free hand slid down her back to shape her rear and pull her against him, leaving her in no doubt of his growing arousal. With Gabriel she felt truly alive, aware of every sensation. The fierceness of his desire was a powerful aphrodisiac, heightening her own. He made her feel whole, complete, and so wanted. Needing to make him feel the same way, to reassure him and prove to him how special he was, she took over, pushing him back until he was lying on the floor beneath her.

She sat up and went to work on his clothes, glad they had left lamps on in the room so she could see him as she slipped each button free before he impatiently pulled off his shirt and tossed it aside. Bending to him, she took her time working down his torso with her mouth and fingers, lingering over his nipples, then his navel, his muscles rippling and tautening, before licking down to the waistband of his jeans.

'No. Let me,' she demanded, pushing his hands away when he moved to undo his belt.

With a groan, Gabriel surrendered to her and she teased him, fondling the hard length of him through the soft, worn denim. 'Lauren,' he growled in warning.

Smiling, she unfastened his belt, then unsnapped the jeans and lowered the zip as slowly as she could, her own aching desire increasing with every moment. He raised his hips to aid her as she skimmed down his jeans and briefs. Once he was naked, she revelled in enjoying his body, in bringing him pleasure, encouraged by the sounds he made, the way his body shifted restlessly beneath her.

'Lauren…'

This time her name was a plea on his lips as she took him to the brink of his control. Nuzzling against him, she breathed in his warm, earthy male scent. She wanted to savour him for hours, as he did with her, but already she was as impatient as he was and could no longer deny herself. She needed him so badly. Hastily dispensing with her own clothes, she took the condom he'd carried in the pocket of his jeans, controlling her eagerness long enough to torment him as she rolled it on, earning herself another threat of retribution. The kind of sensual threat she loved. Sliding over him, she wasted no more time and welcomed him fully inside her.

His hands stroked her with a reverence and tenderness that brought a rush of emotion, making her acknowledge how deep her feelings for this special man had become. Taking her by surprise, Gabriel sat up, pulling her close. Sitting in his lap, she wrapped her legs around his hips, pressing her body against him. They rocked together, sharing slow, deep kisses, their hands caressing. The firelight flickered over their joined bodies as they moved in unison, their rhythm increasingly urgent. When, eventually, they drifted down from the giddying height of passion, reaching a new pinnacle of pleasure, they remained locked in each other's arms, cuddled up in front of the fire under the fleecy throw Gabriel had pulled off the sofa to cover them.

The evening had been the most intimate she had ever known, not only in the intenseness of their love-making but in the sharing of confidences and baring of souls. They had each revealed a part of themselves in a way they had never done with anyone else, which said much about the level of trust between them. She had told people about the adoption thing, it wasn't a secret, but she had never discussed her innermost feelings about it, not even with Chloe. Only with Gabriel.

Holding him tight, she nestled against him, turning her face into his neck. She had never felt closer to him than she did at this moment. Gabriel cared about her, she knew that, but she could no longer pretend to herself that her own feelings stopped there. She loved this man, totally and completely. Knowing what he faced in France, what decisions he had to make about his future, troubled her…both for his own peace of mind and for whatever might lie ahead for them as a couple.

But she couldn't afford to think about that now. She had agreed the terms. No commitments. Live for today. And she would. She loved him, would cherish every moment with him, would show him in every way she could without words what he meant to her, but she couldn't and wouldn't put pressure on him for more than he could give. For now they had the promise of Christmas alone together and she planned to make it as special and unforgettable as possible. She could only wish with all her heart that the new year and beyond would bring hope and happiness.

Christmas Day brought winter sunshine, pale blue skies and cool temperatures. Kate stifled a yawn and took a sip of strong coffee, hoping it would help her wake up. Jem had been on the go for ages. Although he no longer believed in Father Christmas, he still had all the youthful enthusiasm for the day and had opened his presents with breathless excitement. Fearing her son was missing out without his father—and maybe salving her own inner guilt over his true parentage— she tended to spoil him at this time of year, no matter how hard she tried not to overdo it.

Having wolfed down his breakfast, Jem had raced upstairs eager to try on the new football shirt of his favourite Premiership team that Oliver and Chloe had given him. Kate smiled. Her friends were so generous and always remembered Jem, usually giving him books and CDs which he enjoyed immensely. Her smile faded as she thought of Nick. So far he had not given Jem anything. Not that he was obligated to do so, of course, but she had hoped the effort he had been making to be more friendly to Jem since the flood would continue.

She knew that the whole Tremayne clan were getting together for a big family Christmas this year—the first for a long time. With Jack and Edward now back in Cornwall and settled with their respective partners, and with Lucy and Ben celebrating Annabel's first birthday over the holiday, it was a special time for the Tremaynes. Had it only been a year since she had helped deliver that precious baby in difficult circumstances in a deserted barn during a snowstorm?

A wave of sadness swept through her. She wished Jem could be a part of all that Tremayne love and laughter. But she doubted it would ever happen. If only Nick would acknowledge Jem she would be content. She would even be able to force herself to ignore her own needs, her loneliness, the unrequited love she had harboured for Nick for so many years—as long as her son was happy and secure.

This morning, the plan was for a walk along the beach as Jem was eager to fly the Rhombus Entry stunt kite she had bought him, an inexpensive but longed-for item that had been top of his Christmas wish list since they had watched a display in the summer. The fliers doing elaborate stunts and tricks had allowed Jem to have a go and had recommended the Rombus as an excellent beginner's kite.

Kate was about to go upstairs to get dressed for their outing when the doorbell rang. Puzzled as to who would be calling on Christmas Day, she tightened the belt of her robe, pushed some wayward strands of hair back from her face, and left the kitchen. Chloe and Oliver were away—if her suspicions proved correct, Kate believed they would return with some exciting news—so she was on call for any midwifery emergencies over the holiday. But that would entail a phone call, not a visit to her house.

'Nick!' she exclaimed, shocked to discover who awaited her when she opened the door. She could feel the blush warm her cheeks and cursed herself for responding like some flustered teenager to the very sight of him. It didn't help that she was still in her robe. 'Sorry, I wasn't expecting anyone. Merry Christmas.'

'Good morning, Kate. Merry Christmas to you, too.'

Noting the wrapped gifts he held, she moved back. 'Would you like to come in?'

'Please.' He stepped into the hallway and she closed the door. 'I hope I'm not too early. I wanted to call in before going to Lucy and Ben's.'

'Not at all. Jem's been up for hours, excited to open his presents.'

A smile softened the characteristic sternness on Nick's face. 'I imagine. I hope you don't mind. I've bought him a couple of things.'

'No. That's lovely. Thank you.' Surprised and delighted that Nick had unbent enough to remember his son and think to bring him gifts, she led the way to the kitchen. 'Would you care for a cup of coffee? I'll run upstairs and fetch Jem.'

'All right.'

Her pulse racing, Kate hurried upstairs and dressed hastily, pausing a moment to brush her hair and apply some lipstick and mascara before going to Jem's room. She found him wearing his new red-and-white Arsenal top, absorbed in the football annual that had been a present from Lauren and Gabriel.

'Jem, we have a visitor,' she told him with a smile. 'Can you come down, my love? Then we can take your kite and go for our walk.'

'OK.'

Downstairs, Kate smiled at Jem's excitement when he discovered the identity of their guest and the unexpected presents that awaited him.

'Uncle Nick!'

'Hello, Jeremiah.' Setting down his mug of coffee, Nick held out two neatly wrapped parcels. 'These are for you.'

'Gee, thanks!'

A lump lodged in Kate's throat as man and boy exchanged smiles and she noticed the similarities between them. The same eyes. The same shape to the mouth. The same frown of concentration. Would those likenesses become more pronounced as Jem grew older? Would people begin to suspect who his real father was? Hiding her concerns, she watched as Jem tore off the paper to reveal a fun book of science facts and two of the latest computer games.

'Wow! I love them. Thanks, Uncle Nick,' he gushed, taking the older man by surprise and giving him a hug.

'Happy Christmas, Jem.'

Nick's voice was hoarse as he responded to his son's engaging and instinctive reaction. Looking stiff and uncertain, he rested a hand on the boy's head for a moment, and Kate met his gaze, her own eyes stinging with unshed tears at the confusion and emotion in Nick's. This was more than she had expected and she knew it was greedy of her to wish for more.

'Do you have to leave already?' Jem asked with disappointment as Nick rose to his feet.

'Yes, I'm afraid so.' Nick cleared his throat . 'Um… We're having a get-together at my house on New Year's Eve,' he announced after a moment. 'It will be family and a few friends, including children, so it won't be a late night. If you and Jem would like to come, Kate, you'd be welcome.'

Her heart fluttered at the surprise invitation. 'We'd love to, wouldn't we, Jem?'

'Yeah, that would be great!'

Walking with Nick to the front door a few moments later, Kate hesitated and looked up at him, unable to read the expression on his face. 'Thank you, Nick,' she said, fearing the welter of emotions *she* was feeling were all too apparent.

Nick nodded and stepped outside. Kate tightened her hold on the door as she watched him climb into his car, not looking back before he drove away to be with his proper family. He'd thought of Jem, had made him happy, she told herself as she closed the door. That was the important thing to remember right now.

Half an hour later, they had walked around the harbour and reached the nearly deserted beach. While Jem concentrated on sending his colourful delta-wing kite soaring into the sky for the first time, Kate's thoughts remained grounded and on Nick. He had thought to include them in his gathering to mark the end of a year that had been eventful personally, professionally and for the town as a whole, and for that she was grateful. What, she wondered, would the new year hold for them all?

'Lauren?'

Receiving no answer when he walked into the Manor House shortly after midnight, Gabriel headed to the kitchen, washed his hands and then poured himself a glass of water. Reflecting on the last couple of hours, he gave a rueful shake of his head. This had not been the way he would have chosen to spend New Year's Eve.

His first callout had come late in the evening to a four-year-old girl who had experienced her second severe acute asthma attack in less than a week. Her breathing had finally been eased with the administration of oxygen, nebulised salbutamol and oral prednisolone but, given the child's distress, along the frequency and severity of her symptoms, he'd arranged for hospital admission.

He'd only just arrived home when he had been asked to attend an emergency at the Penhally Arms on the harbour front, where a fight had broken out between two groups of revellers who'd had too much to drink. Taunts had turned to threats and, uncharacteristically for Penhally Bay, a running battle had ensued in the street when the guilty parties had been evicted from the pub. Several people had suffered minor injuries, while two had received more serious stab wounds from broken glass. It had taken a while to sort everything out and to stabilise one of the patients, who had lost a great deal of blood and gone into hypovolaemic shock, for ambulance transport to hospital in St Piran. Gabriel had been thankful to come home and leave the police to handle the aftermath of the trouble.

As promised, he had stopped off at Gatehouse Cottage on the way back to check again that the cats, Cyclops and Pirate, were fine. Oliver and Chloe—who had rung a couple of times during the week, sounding blissfully happy with married life—were due back in a couple of days, ready to face the music about their secret wedding. Gabriel felt sure that everyone would be delighted for them.

Foxy, who was curled up on his beanbag by the range in the Manor House kitchen, stretched and snuffled in his sleep. Gabriel washed up his glass, checked all was secure downstairs and that the log fire had safely burned down with the guard around it before he jogged up the stairs in search of Lauren. Light spilled out from his bedroom across the landing, drawing him onwards. His heart swelled and emotion gripped him at the sight he found when he walked into the room.

Dressed in lilac French knickers and matching camisole— the satin and lace creations far more alluring and feminine in his view than blatant, obvious items like G-strings—Lauren was sprawled face down across the four-poster bed. The lavishly illustrated book he had given her on her favourite artist, Claude Monet, and his stunning garden at Giverny in France, was open in front of her. Smiling, he recalled her reaction when she had unwrapped the book on Christmas morning and discovered the promise that had accompanied it...

'What's this?' she had asked, holding up the sticky note he had stuck on the front with 'IOU' written on it.

'Do you have a valid passport?'

A frown had creased the smoothness of her brow. 'Yes, I think it has another two or three years before it's due for renewal. Why?'

'Maybe we could have a long weekend away together in the spring.' Grey eyes had widened with surprised delight at his suggestion. 'I want to take you to see Giverny for yourself.'

'Do you mean it?'

'Of course, *ma belle*. I've been once. It's beautiful.' It meant returning to France far sooner than expected, but it would be worth it to make Lauren happy, and he wouldn't be near the family home. 'I want to share it with you. We'll go when the gardens reopen in April.'

Tears shimmering in her eyes, she had thrown herself into his arms. 'Thank you, thank you, thank you! It's the best gift ever!' She'd kissed him…then shown her gratitude in wickedly enjoyable ways.

Now he crossed slowly to the side of the bed and discovered that she was fast asleep. She looked adorable. Gently, he eased the book out from under her outstretched hand, marked her page and set it on the bedside chest. He hesitated, looking down at her, loath to wake her but needing her with as much desperation as ever.

She had made this Christmas so special for him. Aside from the Monet book, they had exchanged several gifts, each of them finding a mix of things that were either funny, touching, saucy or thoughtful. But it was the time with Lauren, her warmth, her understanding, her passion, her generosity of spirit, that had been the greatest gift of all. The issues with Yvette, his heritage and his future remained unresolved, but some of his heartache had eased by sharing his fears and his hurt with Lauren.

Turning off the main light, leaving the room illuminated by the rosy glow of the bedside lamps so Lauren could get her bearings, Gabriel stripped off his clothes and returned to the bed. Desire rippled through him as he began kissing his way softly up her silky smooth legs, whispering along her calves and lingering at the back of her knees before skimming over her creamy thighs. Lauren murmured, moving gracefully under him as she gradually came awake. He allowed her to roll over and, sleepy-eyed, she looked up at him with a smile…a smile that was so beautiful, so welcoming and so sexy it almost overwhelmed him.

'Gabe.'

'Hey, sleepyhead,' he whispered, his voice rough with emotion and arousal. 'Sorry I was so long.'

'Are you all right? Was it bad?' she asked, her concern evident.

'It wasn't pretty but I'm fine.'

He sat back on his heels and indulged himself, running his hands up and down her body, his fingertips catching on the lace covering nipples that peaked to his touch. Lauren pulled him back down to her, her kiss hot and intense, matching his own hunger. Her hands glided over him, her touch tender, reverent, setting him on fire. He forced himself to slow down, concentrating on removing her camisole and French knickers, kissing each fragment of flesh he exposed. He felt as if he was unwrapping the most precious gift he had ever been given.

'Please,' she begged, moving against him. 'I want you.'

'Soon.'

He nuzzled against her, wanting to take his time and cherish every inch of her but as needy and impatient as her. The subtle, flowery scent of sweet peas, mingled with her own womanliness, intoxicated him. She was so responsive to his touch. Her body quivered beneath his lips and fingers, and the little purring sounds of pleasure in the back of her throat drove him crazy with want.

'Now, Gabe…'

Succumbing to her pleas, unable to resist her or deny her anything, he gave himself up to the magical passion that grew more intense and fiery and special every time they came together.

An age later, sated and relaxed, Gabriel held Lauren close, arms and legs entwined, as she slept. They had gone into this with the pledge of no ties and no commitments. At one time he would have felt relieved that a woman made no demands, but with Lauren he was disappointed and felt a flicker of unease. He had not been looking for any kind of relationship when he had come to Cornwall but what he'd found with Lauren was unique, and he very much feared that nothing between them was ever going to be as simple as they had both vocalised at the start. Instead, he had the sense that he was at a crossroads in his life and what happened here was going to be far more important and life-changing than he could ever have foreseen.

Each day he fell more in love with her. But he hadn't told her. She'd made it clear there were no expectations and she'd given no indication that what they shared meant any more to her, that she felt more for him. He had ten months left in Penhally…ten months to convince Lauren that they were right together. But before he could pledge himself to her, he needed to settle the family issues that dogged him, as well as decide what to do about Yvette and her demands.

Confiding in Lauren, knowing she believed in him and supported him, had helped him rationalise that he could never give up medicine. She had told him about her adoption but he needed her to show the same level of trust, to face up to the problems with her sight and share it with him. Could she ever do that? Would she?

Hugging her tighter, he let out a shaky breath. As they headed into a new year, filled with new hopes and endless possibilities, he vowed to show her in every way how much he loved her. One day, when the time was right, he would tell her how permanently he wanted them to commit to each other. Until then he could only pray that the future would be kind to them and that Lauren would come to love and trust him, too.

CHAPTER EIGHT

LAUREN stood on the pavement by the construction site where the demolished Anchor Hotel was in the process of being rebuilt and gave her details to the policeman beside her. How did her voice sound so calm when inside she was shaking? She looked at her beloved Renault as it sat by the kerb, the driver's side dented and crumpled. A few yards farther along Harbour Road was another car, its front caved in, its angry and foul-mouthed driver arguing with two other policemen.

'I'm sorry about this,' she murmured as the constable put his notebook away.

'It's not your fault, Ms Nightingale, not according to all the witnesses.' He gestured to the gathered crowds and then to the young man who had hit her. 'Luckily there was an off-duty policeman on the scene or the other driver would have driven off. Turns out he has no insurance and was driving while disqualified.'

Lauren didn't know what that would mean in terms of a claim to repair or replace her car, but apparently everyone was satisfied that she had not been to blame for the accident. Everyone but her. She had finished her morning home visits—her final appointment having been with Harry Biscombe at Gow Court, whose osteoporosis was increasingly trouble-some—and had been returning to the surgery for lunch before her afternoon clinic when the crash had happened. Having stopped at the junction of Bridge Street and Harbour Road, she had pulled out into a gap in the traffic, only to have an oncoming car plough into the side of her. Apart from a few bruises she was unharmed but shaken…and she felt impossibly guilty.

The witnesses all attested to the fact that the young man had been speeding and driving erratically, having almost hit a pedestrian and a parked car farther along the seafront before colliding with her. What Lauren hadn't said, but could not ignore, was the simple fact that she had never seen the car at all. It had come out of nowhere and sideswiped her. Her explanations had been silenced by the behaviour of the young man, his unsuccessful efforts to flee the scene and the discovery that he had no business driving at all taking precedence with the police.

'Lauren!'

Hearing her name and the sound of running feet, she looked round to see Gabriel and Oliver hurrying towards her. Someone must have phoned the surgery, she realised, stifling a groan. The last thing she needed was to have people fussing over her and asking her more uncomfortable questions. However, she couldn't deny how comforting it felt to be enfolded in Gabriel's embrace, and she allowed herself a few moments to lean against him and absorb his strength.

These first months of the new year had been the happiest she had ever known. Everything would have been one hundred percent perfect if only she hadn't had to hide two things…how much she loved Gabe and how frightened she was that her sight was deteriorating further. The night blindness she had managed to excuse and cover up, but the fuzziness, the blind spots and decreasing peripheral vision that had begun to occur in recent weeks terrified her.

'Lauren, *ma belle*, what happened? Are you all right?'

Gabriel demanded, holding her slightly away from him so he could look her over, one hand stroking her hair before his fingers trailed down her cheek. He tilted up her chin and looked into her eyes. 'Are you hurt?'

'I'm fine.'

Gabriel frowned, clearly disbelieving her, and glanced over his shoulder. 'Oliver?'

'Here.' The smile curving Oliver's mouth failed to mask the concern in his brown eyes as he stepped forward. 'Hi, Lauren, how are you?'

'She says she's fine,' Gabriel answered for her, increasing her annoyance.

'I'm perfectly all right and able to speak for myself.'

'OK.' Oliver smiled, but she wanted to stamp her foot as the two men shared a glance before Oliver eased Gabriel aside. 'Let me take a look at you to be sure.'

'For goodness' sake,' she muttered ungraciously, aware that the shock of the crash and the fright about her eyes was making her uncharacteristically grumpy.

'Did you bump your head at all?' he asked her.

'No.'

With a gentle but impersonal touch, Oliver carefully checked her neck for any pain or stiffness. After assessing her pulse and her breathing, he cupped her face and she noted his slight frown as he studied her. What had he seen? She bit her lip to keep from asking, not ready for the answer.

'Do you have any discomfort with this bruising?' Oliver queried, moving on to check her arms and discovering the marks beginning to colour along her right forearm that had taken the brunt of the bang as the driver's door had distorted inwards. 'Any nausea or dizziness?'

'Nothing, really. My arm isn't even sore. Honestly, I'm OK. I was just a bit shaken up.'

'I'm not surprised.' Gabriel stepped close again and slid an arm around her waist, his angry gaze on the young man who was being arrested and put into a police car. 'I'd like a few moments with that driver myself.'

Oliver rested a hand on Gabriel's shoulder. 'Let the police take care of him. There are enough witnesses to make sure he doesn't get away with it and from what I hear, he has no licence or insurance, so he will definitely be charged.'

'I should hope so. He could have hurt or killed someone.' Gabriel drew her closer and she could feel the tension in him. 'Come on, I'll take you home.'

'No, it's OK. I need to go back to the surgery,' she insisted, determined to carry on as if nothing had happened.

Gabriel turned her to face him. 'Lauren, be sensible, you've had a shock. You need to rest, *chérie*—'

'What I need,' she stressed, her anger mounting as she pulled away from his hold, 'is not to be babied and told what to do. I make my own decisions. And I'm going back to work to attend to my patients.'

'Lauren…'

Aware that Gabriel and Oliver were staring after her, she picked up the belongings that had been rescued from her car and walked purposefully along the pavement towards the surgery. She was not yet ready to deal with the consequences of what had happened today—or to face the horrifying truth that the problems with her eyesight were getting worse.

'Leave her for a while,' Oliver advised.

Angry, confused and scared, Gabriel wanted to shake off his friend's hand and rush after Lauren, needing to cuddle her and satisfy himself that she was really all right. The rational part of him accepted the sense of Oliver's words, so he fell into step with him and followed Lauren back to the surgery at a discreet distance. At least he was keeping her in sight.

Her outburst had been so unlike her. She had been genuinely irritated by his concern, while all he had wanted to do was take care of her. The day was mild and the March sunshine gleamed off the lighter streaks in her hair as she moved on ahead of them. Another three weeks and they would be in France for their long weekend. He couldn't wait for them to be alone, away from the usual distractions and demands on their time and energy.

Professionally, things had been hectic since the new year, with the surgery busier than ever. Oliver and Chloe had returned from Scotland to much fuss and celebration of their marriage. Only Nick had displayed any sign of disapproval about the elopement, not that anyone had taken much notice of him because it was clear to everyone how happy the couple were and how perfect for each other.

Some of the pressure had been taken off for all the doctors, the workload easing, especially for out-of-hours and weekend calls, with Dragan Lovak back from paternity leave. Gabriel admired the calm, quiet Croatian and was enjoying getting to know him.

Adrian Wescott, the local schoolteacher with long-term tinnitus, had seen the specialist at St Piran and had been declared a suitable candidate for surgery. The operation to remove the stapes and implant an artificial plastic bone was scheduled for the Easter holiday when Adrian would have time off school to recover and, if all was successful, to accustom himself to his altered hearing before the new term began.

Personally, things between himself and Lauren had been just as blissful as they had at the end of the previous year. If anything they were even closer physically, their relationship more intense, but still neither of them had spoken of the future or their feelings, and Gabriel was becoming edgy as almost half his time here in Cornwall was already over. He'd noticed more small moments of concern with Lauren's sight but she refused to confide in him and that lack of trust hurt.

Gabriel thought back to his talk with Chloe in December and her request that he talk to Oliver if he became worried about Lauren. He'd been worried for a while but... He let out a rough sigh. Maybe now was the time to consult his friend and get some advice.

'Did you notice Lauren's eye?'

Oliver glanced at him. 'The right one?'

'Yes.' Gabriel paused, a frown on his face as he watched Lauren disappear through the entrance to the surgery a few yards ahead of them. 'What did you see?'

'Her eyelid was a bit droopy and I thought I detected a squint I'd not noticed before,' Oliver admitted, his voice serious and concerned.

As if by mutual consent, they slowed their pace, coming to a halt outside the car park and turning to look out over the harbour. 'But you've noticed other things before—about Lauren's sight, I mean—since you've been here?' Gabriel asked, sliding his hands into his trouser pockets.

'Nothing I could be definite about, Gabriel.' Oliver sighed and leaned against the wall. 'As an outsider coming in, I was suspicious about Lauren's supposed clumsiness. Everyone laughed at her mishaps and said she had always been that way. I had a hunch there was more to it...but no facts.'

'Me, too,' Gabriel agreed. 'From the first day I met her I knew she was having trouble with her night vision, but I didn't know if it was a long-standing problem or a symptom of something else.'

'And now?'

Gabriel shook his head. 'I'm still worried. She's definitely night blind but copes well and manages to cover it. I'm sure that's why she changed her work hours. And she never drives after dark now. There have been a few other incidents lately and over the last couple of days I saw what you did with her right eye.' He hesitated but decided to keep his nagging suspicions about today's accident to himself.

'Have you spoken to her about it?' his friend asked, meeting his gaze.

'No. Once or twice I've tried to mention the night blindness, as well as the fact that she's stopped painting, but she gets defensive and changes the subject.' Shifting with restless impatience, he let out a shaky breath. 'I'm scared of rocking the boat, Oliver, of pushing her away if I press too hard. I have a feeling that Lauren is increasingly worried but she's not facing up to the problem.'

Oliver gave his shoulder a reassuring pat. 'I never said anything either, even though I noticed that Lauren didn't judge distances well, that she tripped on kerbs and didn't see things in shadow. I didn't know that had progressed to such serious night blindness, though.'

'So should I wait a while longer?' He looked up and saw the answering worry in Oliver's eyes, as if neither of them wanted to voice out loud the various and increasingly frightening explanations that could be the underlying cause of Lauren's sight problems. 'You think it's right that I don't confront her about it?'

'Until Lauren admits it to herself, she's not going to appreciate or accept anyone else challenging her on it. Especially you.'

'Would *you* try to talk to her?' he asked, knowing he was expecting a lot of his friend.

Letting out a heavy sigh, Oliver ran his fingers through his hair and moved away. 'Damn, Gabriel.'

'Please. I'm worried about her.'

'If the opportunity presents itself, I'll see what I can do,' he agreed with evident reluctance, a warning in his eyes when he turned back to face him. 'But I have to tell you, Gabriel, that if Lauren confides in me as a doctor, I'm not going to break her trust and divulge anything if she asks me not to. Not even to you.'

Gabriel felt rigid with tension, his hands clenched to fists. He wanted to argue, but he knew Oliver was right, knew he would do the same if the situation were reversed—their oath allowed them no other option. 'On a personal level I don't like it, but I understand. And I'd just be relieved to know that Lauren was getting some help.'

'I know it's difficult.' Oliver's smile was sympathetic. 'If the chance arises, I'll be advising her to talk to you—count on that.'

'Thanks.'

Knowing there was little more he could do right now, Gabriel tried to be satisfied with the progress he had made. At least now he had voiced his fears to Oliver and he knew his friend would do his best. But knowing he wasn't alone in rec-ognising Lauren's problems was a double-edged sword—while it confirmed it wasn't his imagination, it increased the real possibility that there was, indeed, something wrong. Filled with a mix of emotions, he walked back into the surgery with Oliver, planning to check on Lauren before taking his after-noon appointments. For now his most important job was to be there for her, to love her…and hope that she would trust in him.

Lauren hesitated outside Oliver's consulting room, her hand poised to knock on the closed door.

It was early Friday evening at the end of March and the surgery was quiet. Most of the staff were having a farewell drink with practice nurse Eve Dwyer, who was leaving not only the surgery but the country, too, and heading out to Switzerland to marry Dr Tom Cornish. Lauren didn't know the whole story but apparently the couple had been reunited at the time of the October flood and had spent the last few months rekindling their relationship. Now they were getting married in Tom's adopted country where he was based for his work with the international rescue organisation, Deltraron.

Lauren had been for a drink and had said her goodbyes. Oliver, too, had been at the pub but had returned to the surgery to finish some paperwork while waiting for his wife. Chloe was out with Gabriel attending Diane Bailey, the mother-to-be who had been under their joint care since the autumn and who was determined to have her baby at home—a baby that was now on its way. It was the perfect time to see Oliver alone and confide in him. If she could pluck up the nerve.

It was two weeks since the car accident. Two weeks in which Gabriel had been supportive, caring and concerned. He hadn't pressured her at all, had asked no questions, but she feared he suspected things were not right. It had made things tense between them. Physically things were as wonderful as ever, but she'd been more reserved, concerned about what was wrong with her and trying hard to hide it. She felt guilty. Gabriel would be hurt if he thought she didn't trust him. It wasn't that. It wasn't him. She was scared…terrified. How long could she continue to deny the problems with her sight? It was one thing to fool herself, quite another to put other people at risk.

The young driver who had crashed into her was being prosecuted. Not only had he been driving while disqualified and without insurance, but it turned out he had taken the car without permission. Crashing into her had been a minor sideshow compared to the other charges against him. Her car had been towed to a garage and, as nothing vital had been damaged with the chassis frame or alignment, it was being repaired. While she waited for the work to be done, the insurance company had arranged for a rental car for her.

Although the days continued to lengthen and the nights became shorter, she refused to venture out after dark. During daylight hours, she had been too nervous to do more than the basic local travel she needed to see those patients who relied on her for home visits. Even then she was taking extra care and time. It was an impossible situation and one she knew could not continue.

However scared she was, she had to talk to someone—a doctor—and find out once and for all what was wrong with her eyes. She admired Nick, but she couldn't feel comfortable seeing him and discussing something like this. Dragan and Adam were delightful colleagues, but she knew it would be Oliver to whom she would turn. She trusted him. Despite being aware she was putting him in a difficult position, she knew he would not tell Gabriel, Chloe or anyone else anything she told him in confidence.

She was still undecided what to do when the door in front of her suddenly opened and she stepped back with a gasp of shock, her hand dropping to her side and her startled gaze clashing with Oliver's.

'Hi, Lauren. Were you coming to see me?' His easy smile faded as he looked at her. 'Is something wrong, sweetheart?'

Much to her dismay, she felt an uncharacteristic welling of tears. She *never* cried. What was the matter with her lately? 'No, I— Sorry…' Horrified, she heard her voice break and felt the moisture on her cheeks.

'Come here.'

Oliver gently drew her inside his consulting room and closed the door. He led her to a chair and sat her down, pulling another up so he could sit beside her, his arm around her shoulders as he held her close. After pressing a tissue into her hand, he waited in silence while she gathered her composure.

'Sorry,' she whispered again.

'There's nothing to apologise for.' He took her hand, making her feel comforted, safe, less lonely. 'Lauren, anything you tell me in this room is strictly between us.'

His reassurance gave her the courage to speak up, but

also alerted her to the fact that maybe she hadn't hidden her problems as well as she had thought. 'You know why I'm here.' It was a statement, not a question, and he met her gaze steadily.

'I think maybe you are ready to talk about your eyes.'

The words were gentle but she flinched nonetheless. 'How long have you known?'

'I suspected when I first came here last summer that there was more to your mishaps than clumsiness.' He paused a moment, his touch gentle as he brushed her hand. 'There was nothing I could put my finger on at the time.'

'Does everyone else know?'

'I very much doubt it. No one has said anything…except Gabriel,' he added, watching her.

Lauren swallowed against the sudden restriction in her throat. 'What did he say?'

'Just that he'd noticed a few things, including how you have trouble seeing in the dark.' His expression was sympathetic, understanding. 'He's worried because he cares about you, but he knew it would be wrong to pressure you, that you needed to come to terms and ask for help yourself.'

'I see.'

She pulled her hand away and looked down at her lap, toying with the damp tissue. Part of her was relieved, grateful that Gabriel had given her space and not nagged her, but the knowledge that he had guessed all along, had apparently spoken to Oliver about her, made her uncomfortable.

'Gabriel didn't betray any confidences, Lauren. It was a one-off conversation after your crash when we both noticed that your right eye appeared…different.'

'Different how?' She remembered the way Oliver had looked her over, his frown when he had studied her face. At the time she hadn't wanted to know—now she did. 'What did you see?'

'Your eyelid was unusually droopy and you had a squint.'

'Do you think it was caused by the accident?' she asked after a short pause.

Oliver shook his head. 'Gabriel said he had seen it a few days before.' Sitting forward, he rested his forearms on his knees. 'He also knows that, should you ever decide to speak to me, I would never break my word to you, as a doctor and a friend, and tell him anything you asked me not to. Are you going to talk to me, Lauren? I want to help if I can,' he told her, his voice encouraging, cajoling.

'Yes,' she whispered, knowing she had little choice but to see this through. 'But I'm scared.'

'I'm sure you are, sweetheart, but we'll take things a step at a time together. OK?'

She nodded. 'OK,' she agreed, barely managing to get the word out.

'Good girl.' Oliver's smile carried both relief and gratitude for her trust. He crossed the room, returning after a moment to hand her a glass of water before sitting down again and picking up a notepad and pen. 'Now, in your own time, tell me what's bothering you and what's been happening with your sight.'

After taking a few sips of water, Lauren leaned back in the chair and drew in a steadying breath. 'I don't know exactly when I started to notice things or to equate being clumsy with vision problems. It happened so gradually that it crept up on me over years,' she explained, finding it easier to talk as she found her stride and released so many things she had bottled up and hidden for so long.

She was grateful for Oliver's patience. He listened without interrupting, silent yet supportive, as she recalled her clumsiness, her lack of hand-eye co-ordination, which had made her bad at team sports at school, and how the visual problems had grown worse in the last few years, how it was only in recent months that the night blindness had deteriorated so disastrously and how she had stopped painting since the summer when Chloe had noticed differences in her work.

'I couldn't even see it at first.' A fresh wave of emotion hit and she took a few moments to regroup. 'It was only in good light when I really studied the pictures that I saw the new ones were less sharp, less detailed, that I'd missed things not in the centre of my vision, and that there were subtle changes in depth perception.'

'And you can't see anything in the dark now?' Oliver prompted.

'No. It's becoming difficult in shadow, too, even during the day, and my eyes take a while to adjust to sudden changes in light. Even some colours of text on certain backgrounds are hard to distinguish, including the display on my mobile phone.'

He nodded, resting a hand on her arm and giving her a gentle squeeze. 'Can you tell me what it's like now? What can you see? How do the visual disturbances happen and affect you? Are they there all the time?'

'Not all the time. Things come and go, but gradually worsen.' She frowned, trying to explain, to put the vague impressions into words. 'Sometimes it's like a hazy veil is slowly closing in from the sides and I can't detect things on the periphery of my vision. Things are fuzzy at the edges. The central area is really clear, though, and I can see perfectly. I went to the optician last year and things were fine—but he only checked the basic things like reading the charts and I didn't mention the other problems I was having. I know it was silly but I was in denial.'

'Did he check the pressures in your eyes?' Oliver queried, making a few notes.

'Is that the little puff of air that makes you jump?'

Oliver chuckled. 'Yeah. It's a weird feeling, isn't it?'

'Yes, it is.' Grateful for the easing of the tension, Lauren smiled back. 'He said the pressures were normal.'

'Right. That's fine. And these changes you've noticed have been happening over a long time?'

Lauren nodded in confirmation as they recapped. 'For years the differences were so tiny that they scarcely registered and I guess I deceived myself into believing nothing was wrong. And I found ways of working around things, made excuses for misjudging distances or bumping into things. But I'm worried, Oliver. I can't keep ignoring it. I'm frightened I'm going to make mistakes.' She paused and bit her lip. 'Having found out recently that I was adopted, I have no family medical history to draw on. I don't know what's happening to me or what I should do,' she finished, her voice breaking again as she battled a new threat of tears.

'It's all right, sweetheart,' Oliver soothed, drawing her close for a hug. 'You've taken a huge step, and a very brave one, by admitting it and talking about it. You are not alone in this, I promise. We'll find out what's going on.'

'What do you think it is?' she asked, voicing the fearful question.

Oliver hesitated a moment, raising her concern it might be serious. 'It could be one of several things, so let's not get ahead of ourselves. I'm going to refer you to an excellent consultant at St Piran. Professor Murchison is one of the best. He'll talk things over with you and then he'll do some tests and assessments. When we know what he has to say, we can discuss it again and decide what to do. All right?'

'All right.' She accepted a fresh tissue and blew her nose. 'How long do you think it will be before I can see him?'

'I'll arrange it as soon as possible, but the appointment won't be until after your holiday.'

Lauren bit her lip. 'We're meant to leave next Thursday, but—'

'I know it's difficult when you're worried, and you can't

forget about your eyes, but I want you and Gabriel to go to Giverny and have a wonderful, relaxing time,' Oliver insisted.

She wanted that, too, so she nodded her agreement. 'I'll try. Are you sure you and Chloe don't mind looking after Foxy?'

'Of course not. He's much more comfortable with us now,' he reassured her with a smile. 'And he'll be on familiar territory, too. I know none of us meant for our stay at Gatehouse Cottage to last for so long, but it's worked out well so far. You just tell us if you want your space back.'

'No, it's fine. I know all the repair and renovation work after the flood is taking ages, but we agreed it was important to get those in temporary accommodation at the caravan park back into their homes first.'

'Not to mention people like Gertie Stanbury,' Oliver added with an affectionate grin.

Lauren smiled back. 'Yes. She's done well at Tom's place but I know she'll be much happier when she can return to her bungalow.'

'I hear it should be ready in another couple of weeks.'

'Good.' She paused a moment. While not regretting a moment of her time with Gabriel, living with him at the Manor House meant she had seen less of Chloe and Oliver at home. 'There's no hurry on my account for you to move on. I know the cottage in Fisherman's Row won't be habitable for a while yet.'

'I'm not sure we'll move back there. It's a bit small. But we've not found anywhere else we like. We're just very grateful to share with you.'

'Well, I've rather neglected you,' she admitted, colour staining her cheeks.

Oliver chuckled. 'With good reason. Both Chloe and I are delighted to see you and Gabriel so happy.'

'Thanks.' But mention of the man she loved brought a

return of her anxiety. 'You won't tell him anything about my eyes or the appointment, will you?'

'No, of course not.' Frowning, Oliver closed his notebook. 'You have to decide what is right for you but, for what it's worth, my advice is to confide in Gabriel. I know you care about each other. He's already worried and he'll want to support you. You need that support, sweetheart.'

But what if there was something seriously wrong? She and Gabriel had made no commitment to each other and she didn't want him feeling trapped. He had worries of his own, decisions he had to make about his future, and she couldn't add to his burdens.

'Lauren?'

'I'd rather wait, Oliver. Please. I need to have all the facts first, to know where I stand, before I decide what to do.'

'If that's what you want,' he allowed, but she could tell he was disappointed and that he disagreed with her decision. 'I'll contact the consultant on Monday and make the arrangements for you to be assessed as early as possible. As soon as I have a date, I'll let you know.'

A sliver of fear iced her spine. 'OK.'

'The appointment and tests might last a while, so you should be prepared to be at the hospital for a few hours. You'll likely have some drops in your eyes that could temporarily affect your vision, so you shouldn't travel alone.' He paused a moment, watching her. 'If you haven't told Gabriel or Chloe by then—but I hope you will—I'll come with you to the hospital myself. You don't have to handle this on your own.'

What had she done to deserve such wonderful friends? 'Thank you, Oliver—for everything.'

CHAPTER NINE

'IT's even more amazing than I ever imagined! I can't believe I'm really here!' Spinning round, a huge smile on her face, Lauren launched herself into Gabriel's arms and he caught her in a tight hug. 'Thank you *so* much for this.'

'My pleasure.'

And it was. Seeing Lauren so relaxed and happy and engaged was all the reward he needed. With reluctance, Gabriel released her, contented to follow when she took his hand and led him off around Monet's famous garden. This was her moment, her day, and it was a joy to share it with her.

They had flown from Bristol to Charles de Gaulle airport in Paris on Thursday morning. After spending a couple of hours in the city so Lauren could enjoy some of the sights, they had driven their hire car north-east to the hotel where they were staying for their long weekend. Situated in a stunning eighteenth-century chateau an hour from Paris and twenty minutes from Giverny, the hotel was in a beautiful and peaceful setting, the staff friendly and discreet.

Today, Friday, with the weather exceptionally mild for early April, they were enjoying their visit to Claude Monet's home. Parts of the restored pink-painted house with its green shutters had canopies along the veranda covered in swathes of lushly leaved climbing roses that would look spectacular when in flower. The main gardens were full of spring colour, the borders packed with tulips, narcissi, forget-me-nots, aubretia, fritilaries and pansies, with irises, geraniums and other perennials coming through, along with the soon-to-flower wisterias, clematis, rambling roses and yellow laburnums, which draped over arches and pergolas. Cherry and crab-apple trees were also in bloom and looked magnificent.

Lauren chattered freely and he was happy to listen, to live the experience through her. As she made notes and sketches and took endless photos on her digital camera, he indulged himself and watched her, unable to banish his concern about her behaviour since the crash. Physically she appeared fine, but... He frowned. She'd been different these last days, distracted and distant.

Things had been hectic at the surgery. He'd been out almost all night the previous Friday, missing Eve Dwyer's farewell as he and Chloe had worked together to bring Diane Bailey's second daughter safely into the world. He'd arrived home in the early hours to be welcomed to bed by Lauren who had made love to him with an almost frantic urgency. He still sensed that desperation and restlessness in her and he hoped their few days away would enable him to get to the bottom of what was driving her.

'Can we go and find the Japanese water garden?' Lauren asked, pausing to consult her map of the site.

'Of course.' He brushed a few strands of caramel-coloured hair—the natural blonder streaks shimmering under the spring sunshine—back behind her ear, then dropped a quick kiss on her smiling mouth. 'We have to go through the underground passage to the other side of the road.'

'Great!'

Her enthusiasm was infectious and her delight at finding the famous waterlily pool with its weeping willow trees and the graceful wooden bridge, so familiar from Monet's paintings, filled him with warmth and love.

'It's a shame we're too early for the waterlilies themselves, but it's just magical here, Gabe,' she murmured, awe in her voice as she snuggled close to him.

'We can come again at a different time of year.'

She didn't respond to the promise with the pleasure he expected. Instead, he felt her tense. She withdrew, using the pretext of taking more photos, but he experienced a real sense of fear, an inner chill, that in some intangible way he couldn't understand, Lauren was slipping away from him.

Giverny was as magical as Lauren had imagined it would be and it was even better to be sharing the experience with Gabriel. He was puzzled by her, she knew, and she tried her best to hide the fact that she was distracted by following Oliver's advice to make the most of this short holiday and set her worries to one side. It wasn't easy.

How ironic that she should be here at this time. The place inspired her to paint but her nerve had failed her because of her vision problems and she had made excuses not to pick up a brush since the previous summer. For the first time, faced with the reality that she might never paint again, she felt grief at the loss of the activity that had been such a part of her. And yet Monet, one of the world's greatest artists, had produced some of his best and most well-known works while living here amidst this landscape he had created and when he'd been suffering from his own loss of sight.

Aside from never-to-be-forgotten memories, she took endless photographs which she would download to her computer so she could share them with Chloe, who was excited and envious of her trip. She would also email some to Vicky, who was currently in California, the latest stop on the band's tour. Not that Lauren had divulged much to her curious and gossipy friend about Gabriel and, with the worrying issue of her eyes coming to the fore, she was even more glad now that Vicky was away and otherwise occupied.

The whole weekend was wonderful. They breakfasted on chilled fruit juice and fresh warm chocolate croissants at the hotel, and she wondered how many miles she would have to jog to burn off all the extra calories when they went back home.

On Saturday they went to the nearby town of Vernon. As well as visiting the museum, which held some of Monet's paintings as well as many other interesting exhibits, they also enjoyed seeing the old mill on the Seine and Bizy castle.

While she savoured every moment of being with Gabriel, exploring the local area or relaxing at the hotel, and making love with fervour every night, Lauren couldn't shake off her edginess. She was aware all the time of the sword of Damocles hanging over her. When she returned to Cornwall on Tuesday, this special time out of time would be over and she would have to face reality…the appointment with the consultant which Oliver had scheduled for the end of the week. An appointment which could reveal the true state of her visual problems.

She loved Gabriel so much, but she couldn't tell him so until she knew what was wrong with her and what, if anything, she had to offer him. For now she would not burden him with her worries and confusion. Not until she knew exactly where she stood and what the future held for her. What if she had some kind of tumour or something? If things were bad, she knew he wouldn't desert her, but that was part of the problem. She wouldn't want him to stay for the wrong reasons, couldn't bind him to her out of pity. Despite how her feelings had changed, they had made no promises to each other and were taking things one day at a time until his contract in Penhally Bay came to an end. *If* her situation proved to be bleak, she would have to set Gabriel free. He had his own issues to face. But the very thought of him no longer being in her life, of never being able to touch him, kiss him or make love with him again, was too painful to contemplate.

On Monday morning, after a lingering shared shower, they were enjoying a walk in the hotel grounds before breakfast and discussing their plans for their last full day in France when Gabriel's mobile rang. Lauren noted the frown on his face when he took out the phone and looked at the display.

'It's François,' he explained, surprise evident in the huskily accented voice that still sent tingles down her spine. 'Sorry, *chérie*, I'd forgotten I had left the phone on. Is it OK if I speak with him?'

'Of course.'

She knew the two men kept in touch but it was unusual for his friend to call at this time of the day, especially when François knew they were having a few days away. Despite Gabriel teaching her some French these last months, she didn't follow much of the conversation, but the changing expressions on his face made it clear that whatever news his friend was imparting was unexpected and of some importance. A flicker of unease rippled through her.

'Is everything all right?' she asked as he hung up but remained rooted to the spot, looking stunned. Closing the gap between them, she took his free hand. 'Gabe?'

He shook himself, his fingers linking with hers as if he needed the contact. 'I don't know what to say,' he murmured, sounding shaken.

'Come and sit down.' Concerned, Lauren led him to a rustic seat on the edge of the woodland path. 'What's happened?'

'I had not told anyone but François my address in England. As you know, I needed space from Yvette and her scheming,' he explained and Lauren nodded, still gripping his hand. 'François had a letter this morning from the firm of solicitors in Paris who did work for my father. They have been trying to find me.'

Lauren frowned. 'Does François know why?'

'Yes…in part.'

'And?' she whispered, the tension growing with every passing second.

Dark eyes focused on her and she saw the whirl of emotion in them. 'And they have found something I should have received two years ago. It was mislaid.'

'Mislaid?' Lauren swallowed, barely managing to force the words out. 'What is it?'

'A letter—to me—from Papa. He didn't forget me, Lauren.'

His shaky smile and the roughness of his voice undid her, and she wrapped him in her arms, holding him tight, hoping and praying that his father's last words would help to ease the pain inside him and provide answers to some of his questions.

'Are you sure you don't mind doing this?' Gabriel asked for the umpteenth time.

They sat in the foyer at the solicitors' office in Paris. He shifted restlessly, anxious about what was to come yet filled with gratitude for Lauren's support. From the moment he had received the news from François, she had been adamant that they change their plans and return to the capital straight away. After a hasty breakfast, they had packed their things and settled their bill with the chateau owner, apologising for their premature departure.

'I don't mind at all. This is important, Gabe,' she reassured him now, her hand resting on his thigh. 'We've had a wonderful time and now we need to be here.'

The sudden events had distracted him from his worries about Lauren, the feeling he had that something was wrong and that, despite their physical closeness, she was emotionally withdrawing from him.

'Dr Devereux?' The receptionist, a trim brunette, claimed their attention. 'Monsieur Picard will see you now. You go up the stairs and take the second door on the left.'

'Thank you.'

'Do you want me to wait here?' Lauren asked.

Feeling uncharacteristically vulnerable and uncertain, he shook his head. 'I'd like you to come with me.'

'No problem.' Rising to her feet, she slipped her hand into his and gave an encouraging squeeze. 'Let's go.'

All too soon they had reached the designated room and were greeted by Monsieur Picard, a dapper man in his early sixties, who welcomed them with a gracious smile, switching to English with ease when Gabriel informed him that Lauren's French was not proficient.

'Please, sit down and make yourselves comfortable. Can I offer you some refreshment?' the man enquired as he took his own chair behind a vast leather-topped desk laden with folders.

'No, thank you.' Gabriel hoped Lauren wouldn't mind him speaking for them. He felt on edge, wanting only to take possession of his father's letter. 'It is pure chance that I happened to be in France when the message came through. I understand you have something that belongs to me.'

The solicitor's expression turned grave with apology and discomfort. 'Yes. And I cannot say how sorry I am. The fault was entirely ours. The envelope was misfiled and only came to light in the last week. We did not have your current address on file, hence the further delay in contacting you,' the man explained.

'And this letter…it is from my father?' Gabriel asked, cursing the unsteadiness of his voice but drawing strength from the way Lauren's fingers tightened on his.

'Yes,' Monsieur Picard continued, opening the file in front of him and withdrawing a white envelope. 'This was meant to be given to you in the event of your father's death.'

Gabriel's hand shook as he took the envelope the solicitor handed to him. 'Thank you.'

He looked down at it, saw his name typed on the front, and

was filled with a mix of fear, hope and curiosity about what it might contain. The next moments passed in a blur. He signed a release form, then Lauren handled the pleasantries of departure before guiding him out of the building and encouraging him on the short walk back to the hotel they had booked into for their final night in France. Once there, Gabriel sat on the bed and stared at the envelope in his hand.

'Would you like me to leave you alone for a while?'

'No!' Surprised by Lauren's question, he looked up at her and shook his head. 'Please, stay.'

With care, he finally slit open the sealed envelope and withdrew several sheets of thick cream paper. His heart lurched at the sight of his father's familiar large, sweeping handwriting in the dark maroon ink he had always favoured for his fountain pen. A few photographs fell out and he picked them up, shocked to find himself staring at an attractive young woman with long dark hair, a laughing face and wide dark eyes. He turned one over and read the note, name and the date written on the back before passing it to Lauren.

'My mother,' he managed, staring at the other pictures of the same woman with his father as a young man.

'She's beautiful, Gabe.' Lauren's whispered words and the emotion in them brought a lump to his throat. 'You have her eyes…and her smile.'

Scared he wasn't going to hold things together, he sucked in a steadying breath, returned his attention to the letter and read it through. By the end, he was feeling awed and immensely grateful, as well as emotional. He looked back at Lauren, saw the concern and care in her grey eyes, and desperately needed to share with her, and her alone, what he had just learned about his father and himself.

'It's in French,' he told her. 'I'll translate it for you.'

'If you're sure.'

He just hoped he could reach the end without making a fool of himself. 'I am.' That said, he read the letter again, this time aloud…

'My dear son,

'If you are reading this, I am gone, and I did not find the courage or right time to explain things to you in person. I regret that more than words can say.

'Whatever you may have heard by now from Yvette, I hope you will read my side of the story and find it in your heart to forgive me. I loved Angelique, your birth mother, with all my heart. We were so young, barely twenty, yet she was everything to me. She truly was my angel. Despite all the obstacles my family put in the way, we married as soon as we knew you were to be part of our lives. I would have given up everything for Angelique but she died just days after you were born. I refused to lose you, too, but I couldn't manage alone.

'Beside myself with grief, I stupidly allowed my family to take over and railroad me into marrying Yvette—a good business and social match. Yvette promised to raise you as her own in return for the wealth and position the marriage afforded her. There is enough mixed blood in our ancestry that no one questioned your skin being darker than ours. Your grandfather and some of your cousins carry the same Caribbean heritage, as you know.

'The family placed a condition—you were not to be told about Angelique. I was uneasy but weak. I agreed…but have long wished I had not. Yvette was never a good mother and I am so sorry for her coldness to you. She resented you, hated me and the situation. She will try to use my death to tie you to a life not of your choosing. Do not yield, my son. You are a doctor through and through. The estate will survive well in the hands of your cousins and Yvette's welfare needs are guaranteed for life.

'Please…follow your heart. Do not repeat my mistakes and be bound by a false sense of duty to something that will never make you happy or fulfilled. Live your life your way. You have my love and my blessing always. You have so much to give to the sick who need you. Medicine is your destiny.

'Enclosed with this letter are details about Angelique and her origins, as well as some photographs. Although she had no immediate family left when she came to France, I am sure you will wish to learn more of your heritage and that side of the family. She was an amazing young woman, full of goodness and love. We both wanted you desperately.

'There is much of her in you. I am so proud of you, Gabriel, and Angelique would be, too. Be true to yourself, my son, and be happy.

'Love always, Papa'

His voice cracking, Gabriel set the letter aside and looked up to see tears streaming down Lauren's cheeks. She rushed across the room and wrapped her arms around him. Taking her down with him to the mattress, Gabriel held on tight, burying his face in her hair, breathing in her scent, giving thanks that she was here.

He felt a huge weight lifting off his shoulders and a new sense of freedom welled within him, a peace he had not known for a long time. It was nearly two years since his father had died, two years in which he had struggled to come to terms with all Yvette had told him. Now he knew the truth. His father had not had an affair. He had loved Angelique. Both his natural parents had wanted him. Thanks to his father's loving words, the road ahead was clear to him. Being a doctor was a fundamental part of who he was. His father had known that, had released him from any misplaced family duty and urged him to follow his own path.

Despite Yvette's belief, family responsibility was not something he took lightly. He valued his upbringing, the benefits he'd enjoyed, his father's love. Learning that his father had been proud of him and respected his choices brought a rush of emotion to his heart. His father had known what would happen, had wanted to prepare him, to protect him in death, as he had in life, from Yvette's bitterness and spite.

Thank goodness Lauren was here with him. Natural, earthy, intelligent and genuine, she had given him so much in every way. And she responded to his touch like no other woman he had ever known. She shifted, pulling back to meet his gaze. Touched by her concern for him, he brushed away the tears that showed how much she cared. He loved her so much and valued her opinion above all others. She accepted him for who and what he was, the whole person, not his family name or his bank balance or the ancestral estate. From the first he had sensed Lauren was a kindred spirit. It had been like a meeting of souls.

'I'm so glad for you, Gabe,' she told him, her voice thick with emotion. 'Listen to your father—and to your heart.'

It was good advice. And he planned to follow it. 'Right now my heart is telling me to take you to bed,' he murmured huskily, delighting in the way her eyes flared with answering desire.

Late that night, cocooned in the privacy of their room, the noises of the city filtering up from the streets below, Gabriel held Lauren close, their bodies tangled together, limbs entwined. It had been an unforgettable day…a day in which he had been given a new lease of life and had recaptured his true memories of his father.

His thoughts turned to Lauren. Their love-making remained as passionate and explosive as ever and yet he still sensed that new desperation in her. He needed to tell her how special she was and how much she meant to him. He had held back for so long, scared to push too soon or too hard—in the same way he had given her space to come to terms with the problems with her sight.

Stroking her satiny hair, breathing in her scent, he tightened his hold. 'I love you, Lauren, *ma belle*,' he whispered against her skin, knowing she was not yet asleep.

He fought against the heartache that gripped him when there was no response to his admission bar the tensing of her body. Fear clenched his stomach. Today Lauren's support and reactions had proved that she cared, too, and yet she refused to acknowledge what was between them. Why? What was holding her back? For days he had sensed the times when she had been distancing herself, backing off from him emotionally, and he didn't know how to stop it.

He couldn't force her to trust in him, to love him, but he wanted so much more than the commitment-free relationship they had discussed at the beginning. He *wanted* commitment, *needed* Lauren in his life—for ever. How ironic that at the very time he should have rediscovered his father and be in a position to not only understand his mother's heritage but to be free to plan his future, the one person he wanted most to share it with him was slipping out of his reach.

Lauren sat in Oliver's car on the journey back from St Piran Hospital on Friday afternoon frozen with shock and despair. She bit her lip, trying not to think of the last hours and all the tests she had undergone—a battery of assorted eye-function tests and examinations, including visual field, acuity and colour assessments. There had been a blood test, an electroretinograph—which determined the function of the photoreceptors in the eye—and endless questions. Unfortunately, due to her adoption, she had not been able to provide any details of her family medical history.

Oliver had reassured her several times about Professor Kieran Murchison's reputation and the rotund, balding and jovial man had lived up to his billing today, showing a kindness that matched his thoroughness. Yet he had held her fate in his hands and she had felt sick to her stomach when he had finally delivered his verdict.

'I'm sorry to keep you waiting so long, my dear, but I wanted to be very sure of the results,' he had told her when she had been shown into his office, leaving Oliver—who had stuck with her throughout and had borne the delays and boredom with amazing fortitude—sitting outside in the waiting area.

'But you have the results now?' Her voice had wavered alarmingly. 'What's wrong with me?'

His expression serious, the professor had looked down at her notes before speaking. 'I'm afraid you have a condition called retinitis pigmentosa.'

'What does that mean?'

'It's a group of related, inherited disorders—a genetic disease of the retina—the majority of which have no known genetic cause. The most common cases of RP result from abnormalities of the photoreceptors—the rods and the cones,' he had explained. 'The presentation of your symptoms suggests that you have autosomal dominant RP, which means that you fall into the group who have rod-cone dystrophy, affecting the rods more than the cones. This explains the problems you have reported, including those with your night vision, peripheral vision, bumping into things, slow adjustment to light and so on.'

Struggling to take it all in, Lauren had forced herself to ask the next question. 'What about treatment?'

'There is much we can do to help you manage the condition, and to prepare and cope for the changes that lie ahead. There are various genetic and stem-cell studies ongoing around the world which might have positive results in future, even a bionic eye project. For now, though, Lauren, there is no treatment and no cure. Progression of RP is different for everyone. Yours has been slow so far. Hopefully it will continue to follow the same pattern. You have a challenging time ahead, but it's not a death sentence. And it's not going to happen overnight. So much will still be open to you.'

The words rang in her ears even now. She had a whole stack of advice leaflets to read, a list of recommended books and website addresses to gain further information, but the appalling and impossible truth could not be ignored. Retinitis pigmentosa was a progressive disease. She would continue to lose her vision and, ultimately, could become totally blind.

Her mind in turmoil, she leaned back and closed eyes still blurry from the drops Oliver had warned her would be administered. Aside from the utter terror of today, of facing up to the reality that all was not well with her eyes, she couldn't get Gabriel out of her thoughts. France had been amazing, she'd loved her time away with him. The icing on the cake had been learning about the letter and seeing the difference his father's words, love and pride had made to him, to his sense of identity and his thoughts for the future.

On Monday night in Paris she had frozen when Gabriel had told her he loved her. She had wanted to turn in his arms and kiss him, to shout from the rooftops that she loved him, too, but instead she had pretended to be asleep and had ignored his longed-for words. If only they had come at a different time and not while she'd had this problem hanging over her and had been rigid with fear for her future. A future that now stretched ahead of her, painful and lonely, because Gabriel could not be part of it.

He had been hurt by her silence and there had been an uncharacteristic tension between them on their journey back to Cornwall the next day—a tension that had continued throughout the rest of a busy week. No matter how much she told herself she was doing the right thing, guilt weighed heavily upon her. She hated deceiving Gabriel and keeping things from him. He'd be so upset if he knew where she had been today. And he'd believe she'd kept it from him because she didn't trust him. Which wasn't true. Far from it. She was just so terribly scared about what was happening to her and devastated now that the diagnosis confirmed the worst.

'Lauren? Talk to me,' Oliver cajoled, taking her ice-cold hand in his as he drew the car to a halt outside Gatehouse Cottage. 'What do you want me to do?'

'I don't know. I can't think at the moment.'

His fingers squeezed hers and she heard the shock and upset in his voice. 'I'm so sorry, sweetheart. I'm here for you. We all will be…if only you will let us.'

'I need some time to decide what to do,' she whispered after a long, uncomfortable pause. 'Promise me that you won't say anything to anyone. Not even Chloe. Especially not Gabriel.'

'I've already told you I won't break your confidence, Lauren. But I have to say I think you are wrong to shut out those who care so much about you,' he advised gently.

Shock, anger and fear made thought and reason impossible. Withdrawing her hand from his, Lauren gathered up her things and reached to open the door. 'I can't thank you enough for all you have done for me. I'm more grateful than you can know. But I need to handle this my own way, Oliver,' she told him, her voice quiet but firm.

'All right.' He sighed, running his fingers through his hair, his frustration and concern clear. 'You can always come to me at any time if you want to talk about things, or if there is anything at all I can do. Promise me that much.'

'I know. I promise.'

'I don't like to leave you alone,' he protested, his voice

heavy with worry. 'But Adam swapped with me and I have to get back to the clinic to take evening surgery.'

'Go. Please. I'll be fine. I need to read up, to absorb all the professor said,' she reassured him, holding on to her composure by a tenuous thread.

After Oliver had finally been persuaded to leave, Lauren went inside and wandered around the cottage that no longer felt like home. Home was with Gabriel. A place she could no longer be. She sat down on her bed, Foxy's head in her lap, the booklets describing her disease spread around her, and cried for all that was lost. Everything seemed too monumental to cope with. How long could she continue to do her job? What was going to happen to her one, five or ten years down the line? Would she be totally blind?

The first most pressing and impossible thing she had to do was to distance herself from Gabriel, to begin the terrible process of withdrawing and ending their magical relationship. Even thinking about it brought more pain and sadness than she had ever known. It cut deep inside her. But she had to do it. For his sake. Because he deserved someone who could be his equal, someone with whom he could have a family. With her condition, genetic testing might show she could never risk having children of her own.

Hearing Gabriel's car going past in the drive, Lauren left Foxy behind at Gatehouse Cottage and walked slowly to the Manor House. For endless moments, scared of what was to come, she hesitated on the steps, shivering despite the mildness of the late afternoon. Finally, unable to delay the inevitable, she rang the doorbell. After a few moments, she heard Gabriel's steps jogging down the stairs, then the front door swung open. All the breath left her lungs in a rush at the sight of him. He was so gorgeous. More than anything she wanted to throw herself into his arms, confess all, tell him she loved him, but it wasn't fair to him.

'*Chérie*, what are you doing?' he asked with a laugh, reaching for her. 'Did you lose your key?'

Evading his touch, she stepped back and shook her head. 'No. I—' She broke off before her voice cracked, seeing the smile leave his face, doubt and fear dimming the light in those glorious dark eyes.

'You are scaring me, Lauren. What is it?'

'I need some space—some time to think,' she began, cursing her lack of decisiveness.

Gabriel frowned. 'Space?'

'Yes.' Wringing her hands together, she took another step away, trying to find the strength to do what she believed was right.

'To think about what?'

'I'm going back to the cottage, Gabriel. We've had a great time, but we said no promises, no ties, and I think we need to cool things. You've sorted the situation out now about your father,' she rushed on, her heart breaking at the hurt disbelief on his face. 'You're free to plan your future, to find out about your mother's heritage, to go where you like with your work. The last thing you need is to be shackled to anything or anyone.'

Anger mingled with the pain in his eyes as he looked at her, roughly thrusting his hands into his trouser pockets. 'Don't make this about me, Lauren. Don't make excuses. You had to know how much more this had become. It was never some casual fling. Not for me. I had thought not for you either,' he challenged, his accent more pronounced with his hurt disappointment. 'Or have the last months been nothing but a game to you?'

'No, but…' He had cut her to the quick and she had no way to defend herself so she fell silent.

'I love you, Lauren. I want to make a commitment to you, to marry you. But that clearly means nothing to you and you don't feel the same for me. You've been pulling away emotionally for days. Just have the guts to say so.'

'OK.' She swayed, fearing she was going to collapse in a pit of pain. Nothing had ever been this difficult and she couldn't bring herself to look him in the eye. 'You're right. I can't commit like that.' Her voice wavered as she told that fragment of truth. She couldn't commit but she couldn't tell him why…because she loved him heart, body and soul and couldn't burden him with a blind wife. 'I'm sorry.'

'You're sorry? Is that meant to make this right?' he demanded with an anger she had never heard from him before.

Tears stung her eyes. 'No.'

'You've made your decision, Lauren. There's nothing else to be said.'

Rigid with tension and with a quiet dignity that cried out with his pain and twisted the knife inside her, Gabriel closed the door, shutting her out of the house and his life. The tears fell then, hot and heavy. Selfishly, she wanted to call him back, to pound on the door, to tell him it was all a mistake and explain everything. She needed him, wanted him, couldn't face this without him—but she couldn't manipulate him that way, not after all he had been through with Yvette.

She thought of all he had said, words that should have made her joyous, not despairing. Gabriel loved her. It was what she'd wanted most. But for his sake she had had to reject that love—the most precious of gifts. She didn't deserve him. Pressing a hand to her mouth to mask the sound of the sobs that racked her body, she turned and stumbled back down the driveway, praying that Oliver and Chloe would not be back yet.

She had achieved what she had set out to do. Now her future stretched ahead of her—cold, dark and full of fear. A future that was going to take her sight, her job, her hobbies, her independence. Even that didn't seem to matter as much as what she had already lost. Gabriel…the only man she had ever loved.

CHAPTER TEN

'I'M GOING for a walk,' Lauren announced, unable to bear the atmosphere in the cottage any longer and needing to be alone with her thoughts. 'I'll take Foxy down to the beach.'

'Whatever.'

Chloe's response, while not unfriendly, left Lauren in no doubt that she remained in her friend's bad books and was not to be forgiven any time soon. Smothering a sigh, knowing it was her own fault for not following Oliver's advice and confiding in the people who cared for her, she attached Foxy's lead and let herself out, the Saturday morning sunshine failing to raise her spirits.

She had no idea how she had lived through the last week. Nothing had been this painful and no matter how much she told herself that hurting Gabriel now was better than condemning him to a hopeless future with her, it didn't help. She couldn't sleep, couldn't eat. People were shocked and surprised by the break-up. However many times Lauren trotted out the same excuse—that things had run their course and she and Gabriel had decided to go their separate ways—the telling never became easier, the lie sticking in her throat, multiplying her agony.

She couldn't avoid contact with Gabriel at the surgery. The sight of him, proudly dignified yet so obviously unhappy, ripped at her shredded heart. How she was going to bear the situation for the remainder of his time in Penhally she didn't know—seeing him every day, not being able to touch him, barely speaking unless it was with strained politeness about work. But the very thought of him leaving for good, of never seeing him again, or hearing his softly accented voice and rumbly laugh, was impossible to contemplate. No matter how much she kept convincing herself she was doing the right thing for Gabriel's sake, the temptation to be selfish and go to him to confess all never diminished. Indeed, it increased with every hour that passed.

Desperate to escape the pain of losing Gabriel and the anxiety over her diagnosis, she had thrown herself into her work, all the time wondering how long she would be able to do her job and how soon she would have to stop driving completely. Yesterday she had taken Paul Mitchell and his mother on their once-a-month trip to a local private spa that made their hydrotherapy pool available by appointment for patients with special needs. The water-based exercise she was able to do with him was good for Paul with his Duchenne muscular dystrophy.

Some long-term patients she had seen during the last twelve months had been signed off, Mike Trevellyan among them. As well as cases which turned around fairly quickly, like Zena with her sore neck and Dan Somers with his hamstring injury, she had all her regulars, including Harry, Edith and baby Timmy Morrison. Stella Chamberlain's Parkinson's disease was still keeping her in the Harbour View Nursing Home, while Gertrude Stanbury was looking forward to returning to her bungalow in Gull Close in the next week. Neither the anticipation of going home nor her painful arthritis diverted Gertrude from commenting on what she viewed as Lauren's stupidity in letting Gabriel get away.

At home she had Chloe on her case and she recalled her

friend's initial reaction when she had learned of the break-up. 'You said to me in the summer to grasp what I had with Oliver, that something that special, some*one* that special, doesn't come along often in life. You and Gabriel are special, Lauren. He loves you, and I'm sure you love him. Why are you throwing it all away?'

'You don't understand.' And she hadn't been able to explain.

'No, I don't. Neither does Gabriel. He's confused and distressed. You've really hurt him. You owe him more than that.'

Lauren had spent as much time in her room as she could, avoiding Oliver and Chloe. She'd studied the leaflets the professor had given her, looked up information on the Internet and read a couple of biographies written by people who were living with retinitis pigmentosa. It was all depressing but moving. She hoped she could be even as fractionally as brave and resourceful as those whose stories she had read—stories which had scarily mirrored many of her own experiences. With time she hoped to come to terms with it, to make plans, to find some courage to cope with whatever was thrown at her, but the shock still lingered, as did the gut-wrenching ache of missing Gabriel every minute of every day.

Leaving the quiet country roads, she headed down through the town towards the harbour front. All she could do was tell herself she was making the best choice for Gabriel in the long run. He'd had enough of manipulative women in his life. She couldn't tie him to her out of duty or because he felt sorry for her. But it was almost impossible to let go. Nothing had hurt this much. When his time here was over, he would go back to France and no doubt settle down one day and have a family of his own. She couldn't allow him to take on a wife who was slowly but surely losing her sight, who might be a genetic risk and unable to have children, and who, at some time down the line, could be blind and dependent in more ways than she could bear to comprehend.

Despite feeling as if she was slowly but surely unravelling, somehow she had to try to survive this torment. One day at a time.

With one more house call left to make on Saturday morning, Gabriel sat in his car outside the patient's home, his arms folded on the steering-wheel, his head resting on them. A week and a day on and he had still not recovered from the shock of Lauren's words. One day he had been given the gift of his father's love and approval, the identity of his birth mother, and had felt his life was finally getting back on track again, but shortly afterwards Lauren had dropped her bombshell, rejecting his love and breaking his heart in the process.

What had he done wrong? Had he taken Lauren for granted? Had he been mistaken that she returned his feelings? He still didn't understand how she could have walked away as if there was nothing at all between them. It hadn't been just sex. Lauren could deny it all she liked but he wouldn't, couldn't, believe she felt nothing, that all they had shared had been meaningless fun. He was sure he hadn't misjudged things that badly. What they had was special, explosive, a once-in-a-lifetime connection...a connection that had hit them both the moment they had met. He had never felt like this about anyone else. Had never hurt so much. He couldn't sleep without Lauren in his arms, couldn't eat, was barely getting through each day.

Even the letter from his father had failed to distract him for long, despite the searches he had done on the Internet to learn about Martinique, where his mother had come from. One day he hoped to go there, to find out more about his roots, but he couldn't get excited about it now, could do nothing but yearn for Lauren.

With a deep sigh, he climbed out of the car, collected his medical bag, and walked to the front door, reviewing what he knew about the woman he was going to see. Delia Rocco was only thirty-two and had suffered a serious stroke ten days ago. She had been discharged from hospital the previous day and he was doing a follow-up visit to ensure she and her husband were coping. He hadn't wanted to leave them all weekend without support, and he needed to discuss Delia's needs—which would include physiotherapy and necessitate him facing Lauren. His gut tightened with pain.

Delia's husband, Neil, answered the door and invited him in, a tired smile on his face. 'Thanks for coming, Dr Devereux.'

'No problem. How are you both doing?' he asked, knowing that Neil was going to need as much understanding and support as Delia. 'Relieved to be home?'

'Very. But it's scary, too, not having the nurses on hand,' the man admitted.

'That's understandable, but I'm sure you'll do fine, and don't forget you have the doctors, district nurses and physiotherapist from the surgery willing to step in whenever you need us.'

Looking reassured, Neil relaxed. 'Thank you. Well, I expect you want to see Delia first?'

'Yes, please. Then we can have a chat.'

Talking with and examining Delia revealed that she had been left with weakness and reduced movement down one side of her body and her speech was slurred. Given the severity of her stroke, she had done well to make so much improvement so quickly, although she had a long haul ahead of her. She was brave but clearly bewildered at having been struck down at such a young age, scared about what the future would hold for her. Gabriel determined to do the best he could for the couple to ensure they had something positive to look forward to.

'I'm just so grateful Delia is still here and recovering,' Neil said a while later, holding his wife's good hand. 'Life without her would be intolerable. She tried to send me away, of course, but I wasn't having any of it.'

Puzzled, Gabriel frowned. 'Sorry? Send you away?'

'I was so scared, so confused. I got it into my head that Neil would be better off without me, that I would be a burden to him and prevent him having a normal, happy life,' Delia explained, taking time to try to enunciate each word.

'She said she didn't love me any more, that she didn't want me,' Neil confirmed with a rueful smile. 'I almost believed her at first, I was under so much stress and so worried about her, but thankfully I saw through what she was doing.'

With a start, Gabriel sat back, his thoughts on Lauren. Frowning, he thought over the sudden way she had ended things with him. Was there more behind it than he was seeing? Unsettled, he began packing his things away and returned his attention to Delia and Neil.

'I'll see you again next week. But call any time if there is anything you need,' he advised them. 'Our physiotherapist, Lauren Nightingale, will come to see you on a regular basis and work out an exercise and therapy schedule with you.'

'Thanks. How is Lauren?' Neil asked.

Pain lanced through his heart. 'Fine, as far as I know. She's an excellent physio, so you'll be in good hands.'

'Oh, I know that,' Delia confirmed with a lopsided smile. 'I was a couple of years ahead of her at school. She was always very caring to people.'

'I was just concerned because I saw her at St Piran Hospital last week when I was waiting for Delia. Lauren didn't see me, but she looked upset,' Neil clarified.

Lauren had been at the hospital? Upset? Every part of him went on high alert. 'When was this?' he asked, trying to keep his tone casual.

'Last Friday afternoon. They'd taken Delia down for some

eye tests,' he added, clearly unaware of the turmoil Gabriel was experiencing.

Dieu! Why hadn't he considered it before? He thought of the timing. Lauren had been to the hospital and that same night she had broken up with him. What on earth had she found out? Fear gripped him. Had Lauren reacted to the shock as Delia had, pushing away those close to her because she felt she would be a burden? He had to know, had to find out.

Taking his leave of the Roccos with as much speed as was polite, he rushed back to the surgery where Oliver was taking the Saturday morning clinic. Hippocratic oath or no Hippocratic oath, he was going to get some information from his friend.

'Is Oliver still with patients?' he asked Sue when he arrived back at the surgery and handed over his tray of patient notes.

'No, the last one left about five minutes ago,' she confirmed. 'Everything OK?'

'Mmm? Oh, fine. I need to see Oliver.'

Leaving a surprised Sue behind him, he hurried to his friend's consulting room. The door was closed, so he knocked and waited impatiently, just in case Sue was wrong. Despite his urgency, he wouldn't embarrass or upset a patient.

'Come in.'

Oliver was alone, he discovered, writing up his notes. He swung his chair round, a wary expression on his face as Gabriel closed the door and crossed to the desk.

'I know you can't break a confidence, Oliver, but I want to know what's going on with Lauren,' he began, pacing out his frustration. 'I love her, I want to marry her. When she broke things off, it nearly killed me. Someone told me they saw Lauren at the eye clinic last week. That same day she told me it was over. I don't believe that's a coincidence.' He paused, considering how much to tell Oliver. 'It's taken a

while to get my head together but I think she has some misplaced idea she's going to be a burden and has to let me go.'

'Gabriel—'

'I *know*,' he cut in with irritation, rubbing a hand across the
back of his neck, feeling the tightness of the tension gripping
his muscles. 'I know you can't tell me outright. But you can
give me a clue.'

Oliver regarded him for a few moments in silence. 'For what
it's worth, I've tried several times to get Lauren to confide in
both you and Chloe, but I have to respect her wishes.'

'Whatever it is, however bad, I'm not leaving her, not
giving up on her. Am I on the right track? Or does she really
feel nothing for me? Give me something to work on. Please.'

'You don't make things easy, Gabriel.'

'How would you feel if it was Chloe?' OK, he wasn't
playing fair, but he was desperate. 'If Lauren thinks she's
doing this for my benefit, she's wrong. If she cares about me,
she'll thank you in the long run.'

Oliver closed his eyes and sighed, running his fingers
through his over-long hair. 'I can't give you any details, but
you're right, Lauren's pushing everyone away because she
thinks it's the right thing to do.'

Sitting down because his legs felt too shaky to hold him
up, Gabriel met Oliver's troubled dark gaze. 'She's not dying?
It's not a tumour?' He forced the words out, the relief indescribable when his friend shook his head. Sucking in a steadying breath, he pressed a hand over his sternum as he
acknowledged how frightened he had been. 'OK. It doesn't
matter what it is, I want to be there for her. I just wish she had
told me so she hadn't had to face all this alone.'

'She wasn't alone,' Oliver admitted after a moment.

Gabriel glanced up, a mix of emotions rushing through him—
disappointment and annoyance at being shut out, but gratitude
to Oliver for being such a good friend. 'You went with her?'

'Yes. I thought it was the lesser evil. Lauren refused to tell you or Chloe and I knew none of us would want her to go on her own.'

'Thank you for being there for her. Now, it's time I found her and discussed a few things,' he finished, rising to his feet.

'Good luck.' Oliver's smile was wry. 'She can be stubborn when she sets her mind to something.'

'So can I. And now I know what she's up to, I'm not going to let her sideline me again.'

He left the surgery for home, needing to change clothes and then track down Lauren. A shiver went through him as he imagined all she had been through this last week or more. He realised now that the worry of facing up to her sight problems had led to her withdrawal, to her being distracted and to her urgency for physical closeness—especially if she'd feared things would be over when she had a diagnosis. While it pained him that she hadn't spoken to him about it, he understood how fear and anxiety could affect someone's decision-making. Thinking of her frightened and confused and alone brought a lump to his throat. He wished more than anything that he had been there to help her through what must have been a shocking and scary experience. His heart ached for her.

Lauren touched something deep inside him, filling an empty space he hadn't realised he'd had until he'd met her. She grounded him, made him laugh. The last months with her had been the happiest of his life—breaking up more painful than anything he had ever experienced. But now he knew what lay behind her actions and her misguided thoughts he wasn't letting her go—not while he had breath in his body.

'I can do all kinds of tricks with my kite now, Uncle Nick.'

'I'm sure you can,' Nick responded, voice gruff. 'Show me some of them.'

Kate smiled as Jem rushed ahead of them on to the surfing beach below the cliffs and beyond the promontory on which the lighthouse and the church stood. She glanced back at the latter building, wondering what the new permanent vicar would be like, an appointment finally having been made. Whoever took up the role next month would have a difficult act to follow. Reverend Kenner was still much missed.

It was a perfect spring morning, sunny and with a hint of freshness in the air. Nick's suggestion of a walk on the beach had been a pleasant surprise and she had been happy to put off her visit to the Saturday farmers' market so that the three of them could spend time together. Since Christmas, and the successful New Year's Eve party at his house, Nick had made a real effort to play a part in Jem's life. For that Kate was grateful. That he'd made no mention of claiming his son still pained her, but she tried not to be impatient.

They stood side by side, watching in silence as Jem skilfully had his kite soaring into the sky and began performing some stunts.

'He's good,' Nick commented after a while, an enigmatic expression on his face, his hands buried in his trouser pockets.

'Yes.' Kate pulled her gaze away from his profile and looked back at her son with pride. 'He took to it straight away. I'm thinking of getting him a more advanced kite for his birthday.'

'Good idea.'

Nick's tone was cool and she worried that mentioning Jem's birthday had touched on forbidden ground and brought back memories of his conception. She sighed, weary of having to be careful what she said in case Nick took exception to it. Before she could decide whether to call him on it or change the subject, they were approached by an older couple.

'Are you folks local?' the woman asked with a broad smile, her American accent thick with Deep South tones.

'We are.' Aware of Nick's reserve, Kate smiled back. 'Can we help you?'

'Would you be kind enough to take a photograph of us with the lighthouse in the background?'

'Of course.'

Kate was surprised when Nick stepped forward and took the digital camera. While he snapped a few photographs, the man chattered about the legend of the wreck of the seventeenth-century Spanish treasure ship, the *Corazon del Oro*, which lay off the rocks to the north of the lighthouse. Keen not to be left out, Jem ran up to join them just as Nick handed back the camera.

'Thank y'all so much! What a cute family you make,' the woman gushed, beaming at them as she linked arms with her husband. 'Why, the little man is just the image of his daddy!'

The American tourists left and Kate smothered a groan as she glanced at Nick and saw him stony-faced and rigid with tension. Jem, however, laughed.

'She thought you were my dad, Uncle Nick,' he joked, oblivious of the atmosphere as he picked up his kite and prepared to run off again. 'Cool, or what?'

Anxiety gripped her at Nick's expression. She sucked in a breath. 'Look, Nick—'

'No.' He held up a hand and backed away. 'I'm sorry, Kate. I tried. But I can't do this. It's too much.'

Tears stung her eyes, pain lancing through her as he turned and strode off in the direction of his house, leaving her and Jem alone. Again. All the progress of these last months, the new closeness, the joy for Jem, had been stolen in an instant by a stranger's unwitting comments. Clearly Nick wasn't ready. Maybe he never would be.

The knowledge tore at her heart and made her unutterably sad for herself and deeply hurt and angry for Jem, who had asked for none of this. How could Nick reject the boy? She wanted to chase after Nick and make him see reason, but she knew him of old and he wouldn't change his view unless he wanted to. Pushing him further would get nowhere. He had to come to terms and make the decision for himself. And if he didn't? If he could never accept Jem and have any kind of role in his life?

If that were the case, maybe the time had come for her to make a complete break, to think about leaving Penhally Bay and the man she had secretly and hopelessly loved for so long. For Jem's sake she couldn't risk Nick flitting in and out of his life as the mood took him. It would be too confusing for her son. And unfair. Maybe she should admit defeat and make a new life for herself and Jem elsewhere. A life without Nick. As he disappeared from view, her heart ached, and she feared this might well be the end to all her hopes and dreams.

A familiar car drew her attention as it approached the church and parked. Gabriel climbed out and she watched as he walked towards the solitary figure sitting hunched and alone on the rocks by the lighthouse at the end of the promontory. Lauren. With all her heart Kate prayed that the young couple, so right for each other, could find a solution to whatever had caused them to part last week. Their hurt had been palpable. She sent up a wish that Lauren and Gabriel could enjoy the kind of happy ending and life-long love that she herself had been denied.

Her mind full of the tough decisions that lay ahead, Kate turned and went to find her son.

Lauren sat on the rocks by the lighthouse—a favourite place she had often come to paint—and stared sightlessly out to sea. She wore sunglasses, as advised by the professor, to protect her eyes from damaging UV rays…eyes currently blurred and puffy from her tears. She despised self-pity, but she felt so overwhelmed at the moment and liable to cry at the merest provocation. It was very unlike her. But the future seemed so scary, so lonely, so bleak. She was worried about her eyes, about how she would cope when she could no longer work or maintain her independence. And her heart ached for Gabriel and what could never be.

Foxy sat beside her and she hugged him close. When he began whining and struggling against her hold, she pulled back in puzzlement. He strained at his lead, panting as he stared fixedly at something behind her. Lauren glanced round, a gasp of shock escaping, her heart lurching and her body tensing as she saw Gabriel striding towards her. He looked impossibly sexy in well-worn, figure-hugging jeans and his mulberry jumper. The lead slipped through her suddenly nerveless fingers, and Foxy's paws scrabbled for purchase on the rocks as he charged to greet the man whose every step inexorably closed the distance between them.

She watched as Foxy greeted Gabriel with enthusiasm. Clearly the dog had missed him as much as she had. Gabriel hunkered down and she could hear his huskily accented voice, if not his words. She saw him stroke the smooth brindle-and-white coat and her stomach clenched as she vividly recalled what it was like to feel those hands caress her bare skin.

Unable to bear it, she stifled a sob and swung round to face the sea again, trying to tune out Gabriel's voice by focusing on the sound of the waves against the rocks. But the sea was fairly calm today, providing poor entertainment for the surfers and failing to distract her from the man she could sense approaching. She stiffened as he sat beside her, far too close, far too tempting. What was going on? Why had he sought her out?

'Hi. Chloe said you might be here.'

His voice betrayed none of his previous anger and hurt. Indeed, he seemed impossibly relaxed. The same could not be said for herself. She was too aware of Gabriel. His earthy, citrusy fragrance tantalised her. Even across the

small gap that separated him she felt the warmth of his
body—a body every fibre of her being longed to hold again.
Gabriel knew just where to touch, to stroke, to lick to send
her to madness, as she did with him. Her heart yearned for
what she could never have. Shifting restlessly, she kept her
gaze averted, watching as Foxy turned a couple of times and
lay down on a rock in front of them, dozing in the sunshine.
She jumped when Gabriel reached out and captured one of
her hands in both of his, panic rising as he refused to allow
her to pull free.

'It's not going to work, you know, *chérie*.'

The sound of his voice tightened her insides with longing
and his touch made her shiver. Her control deserted her.
'W-what isn't?'

'You…trying to push me away,' he told her, his tone calm
and conversational. 'Pretending you don't feel the same as I
do about what we have.'

'You don't understand. I can't offer you anything,' she
whispered, failing once more to remove her hand from his, his
touch setting of ripples of sensation, weakening her resolve.

'I understand more than you think. And you can offer me
everything, *ma belle*, if only you believe and trust me.'

'Gabriel…'

'It took me a while to work out what you were doing.' He
raised her hand to his mouth, his lips whispering over her skin,
stealing her breath. 'This has been the worst week of my life.
I cannot describe how much I have missed looking at you,
talking with you, making love to you, holding you in my
arms as I sleep.' His tongue-tip teased circles on her palm and
she bit back a whimper, fighting with everything she had to
hold on to her resolve. 'I'm not prepared to be without you
for another minute.' He took off her sunglasses, dark mocha
eyes gazing deep into her own. 'Look at me and say you
don't love me. I know you think you're doing the right thing,

but you're not. Tell me the truth, Lauren, once and for all. Lay it on the line.'

Every part of her was shaking and a tear breached the barrier of her lashes and trickled down her cheek. His thumb caught it, brushing the salty wetness away. It had been impossible enough to end it and send him away that evening outside the Manor House. There was no way she could force the lies out a second time. She felt trapped, desperately wanting to avoid this confrontation but unable to escape.

'I'm losing my sight! Is that what you want to hear?' she cried, all the fear, anger and despair welling up inside her and seeking release in an unstoppable tide. 'I have retinitis pigmentosa. I'm going blind, Gabe.'

'Shh. Come here, *mon amour*.'

Turning to face her, he pulled her close and she collapsed into his arms, sobbing as she buried her face against him. His warm strength enfolded her and she breathed in his scent. One arm held her tight while his free hand stroked her hair, his soothing words calming her. Weak, she allowed herself a few moments to believe everything could be all right, but reality intruded and she pulled back. He allowed her some space but he didn't let her go.

'Gabriel, we can't do this. I—'

'Yes, we can,' he interrupted with steely determination, his fingers gentle as they wiped her cheeks. 'I've known from the first that there was something wrong. The way you walked into things or missed what was in shadow right in front of you. How you unconsciously count your steps in the dark. You stopped painting, sought routines that were familiar, had trouble judging distances.'

'Why didn't you say anything?' she challenged, shocked and upset.

He frowned, a furrow creasing his brow. 'Because I didn't want to lose you by nagging. And you had to come to terms yourself, to recognise and accept, to ask for help.'

'But—'

'Lauren, it doesn't change how I feel about you. It matters to me in the sense of what it means for you and your joy in life, but not for any of the reasons you think.' He cupped her face, forcing her to look at him, to see and hear his sincerity. 'I don't feel pity or duty. Far less trapped. I love you, *ma belle*, no matter what. As the vows say…in sickness and in health, in good times and in bad, for better and worse.'

'You can't want me! I can't let you be burdened with this,' she cried.

For the first time a thread of anger returned. 'What gives you the right to make my decisions for me? To take away my choices? I'm an adult, Lauren, and capable of knowing my own mind.'

'I can't ask you to be tied to this. To me.'

'You are not asking. I am choosing. Of my own free will. Because I love you.' He paused a moment, watching her, considering, thoughtful. 'If it was the other way round, what would you do?'

Lauren licked lips that felt dry and struggled to find her voice. 'I don't understand.'

'If I were the one who faced some kind of illness or had RP, or if I had an accident and faced the rest of my life in a wheelchair, would you walk away and leave me? Would you stop loving me?'

'No!' she exclaimed, fury rising within her. 'Of course not.'

'Then do not expect that of me.'

Her heart stopped. With those words, she truly understood. 'Gabe…'

'I can no more live without you than I can without oxygen,' he told her huskily, drawing her back into his arms. 'You give meaning and joy to my life. You're my friend, my confidante, my lover. I will always love you, no matter what, and I will *not* walk away from you.'

'I don't know what's going to happen to me,' she sobbed, fresh tears threatening.

'I know you are frightened. And angry. It's all so new and confusing and scary. That is normal, human,' he reassured her, hugging her close. 'But I also know your courage and humour and intelligence. Your spirit will see you through. And you won't be alone, *mon amour*. We'll face this together. And together we can do anything.'

She cried again then, releasing all the tension and the fear and loneliness of the last days and weeks as she clung to him. 'RP is degenerative and incurable.'

'No one knows what the future holds. Already there are advances, possible new treatments, encouraging research with stem cells, even prosthetic retinas. However bleak things seem now, a few years down the line it may be different, there may be much that can be done to save, maintain or even improve sight for those with RP. But whether or not that happens, we have our love, our passion, our friendship. Life waits for no one, Lauren. We grasp what we have. We've been blessed to have each other.'

Accepting a tissue, she blew her nose and allowed him to cradle her against him. 'What about a family?' she asked, broaching a subject that disturbed her greatly. 'Professor Murchison said I could have genetic screening but what if the results show I can't risk having children? I don't want you to give things up for me.'

'We'll cross each bridge as we come to it, *chérie*,' he en-couraged, and she marvelled at his calmness, his acceptance. 'You are the person who matters most to me. If we can't have children, so be it. If you wanted to, we could consider adoption—and do it properly so any child knows he or she is loved and all about their roots.'

'I really don't deserve you,' she whispered, overwhelmed by his love and understanding and innate goodness.

With a mock growl he gave her a gentle shake. 'Don't say silly things like that. You are the best thing to ever happen to me.'

'But what about your search for your own roots, Gabe? You can't give up on that, on finding out more about your mother,' she insisted, knowing how important it was to him. 'I don't want to hold you back. And don't you want to go back to France? What about your work?'

'Stop inventing obstacles,' he chided with the kind of rumbly chuckle that warmed her right through.

'I—'

His fingers stroked her face as he hushed her. 'I'm still going to research my mother. I've not decided what to do when my contract here ends, but we'll make that choice together. There are all kinds of options. I just heard this week that Lucy is about to give birth again,' he informed her. 'She wants to stay at home with the children and may not come back to work at the surgery for some while, and then only part time. Maybe I can stay on in Penhally.'

'Really?'

'I love it here.' He dropped a kiss on her forehead. 'The solicitor says that the Bartons have decided not to return to England after all. They are going to put the Manor House on the market when my tenancy ends. We could buy it—leaving Oliver and Chloe to buy Gatehouse Cottage, where they are happy. There are a range of possibilities, Lauren. We can do whatever we want.'

Filled with new hope, she pressed closer to him. 'I don't care where we go or what we do—as long as I'm with you. I'm sorry, Gabe. I thought I was doing the right thing. I love you so much and I thought it was unfair to trap you, that you would have a better life without me being a burden and dependent on you. You'd already been so manipulated by Yvette, I didn't want to do the same thing.'

'I know. You temporarily lost your judgement,' he teased,

nipping her earlobe. 'But I forgive you. We put that behind us now and move on. OK?'

'OK.' A rush of peace flowed through her and she allowed herself to believe that maybe it was going to be all right.

Gabriel smiled and drew her to her feet, taking Foxy's lead in his other hand. 'Good. Now, come with me.'

'Where are we going?'

'Home. To bed. We have a week of loving to catch up on and I intend to make the most of every moment.' The sensual promise in his sexily accented voice sent needy desire coursing through her. 'When we come up for air,' he continued with a wicked smile, 'we can start planning our wedding. We can elope like Oliver and Chloe or we can have a big shindig. Whatever you want. Just so long as it is soon.'

'Is that a proposal, Dr Devereux?'

'It is, Ms Nightingale.' He sent her a mock glare in warning. 'And I don't plan to take no for an answer.'

'Just as well I'm going to say yes, then.'

He caught her to him and swung her round, tangling them up with Foxy. Lauren laughed through her tears—happy tears—beyond grateful that Gabriel loved her, believed in her and hadn't given up on her. The fingers of one hand sank into her hair, tilting her head for his kiss. A hungry, deep, thorough kiss that was full of the passion and desire that had flashed between them from the first moment and the love that had grown with each day that had passed.

Gabriel broke off, his breathing as ragged as hers. She could feel his heart thundering as madly as her own. She could also feel the effect their kiss had had on him as she rocked her hips against his. Sweet mercy she had missed this…missed him…so much.

'Home,' he growled with pleasing desperation.

She wasn't at all sure she could wait to get back to the Manor House. Excitement fired her blood and an ache of need clenched deep in her womb. Some time in the next decade or two she might even manage to breathe again. Filled with the same urgency that drove him, she allowed Gabriel to take her hand, linking their fingers, as they all but ran back to his car.

Anticipation clamoured inside her. How could she have gone from despair to blissful joy in such a short time? The sexual tension crackled between them as they drove back through town—a town that had been through so much in the last year or two but which had only grown stronger and more together because of it.

Just like Gabriel and herself.

The future of her eyesight was uncertain, but with Gabriel by her side and secure in their once-in-a-lifetime love, she would no longer be afraid. Wherever they went, whatever they did, together they had everything they would ever need. Each other…united in body, heart and soul.

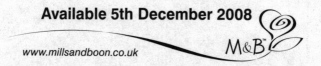

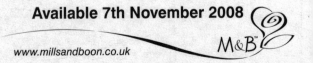

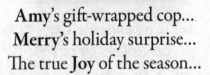

Celebrate 100 years of pure reading pleasure with Mills & Boon®

To mark our centenary, each month we're publishing a special 100th Birthday Edition. These celebratory editions are packed with extra features and include a FREE bonus story.

Plus, you have the chance to enter a fabulous monthly prize draw. See 100th Birthday Edition books for details.

Now that's worth celebrating!

September 2008

Crazy about her Spanish Boss by Rebecca Winters
Includes FREE bonus story
Rafael's Convenient Proposal

November 2008

**The Rancher's Christmas Baby
by Cathy Gillen Thacker**
Includes FREE bonus story *Baby's First Christmas*

December 2008

One Magical Christmas by Carol Marinelli
Includes FREE bonus story *Emergency at Bayside*

Look for Mills & Boon® 100th Birthday Editions at your favourite bookseller or visit
www.millsandboon.co.uk

0908/CENTENARY_2-IN-1

310

FREE

4 BOOKS AND A SURPRISE GIFT!

We would like to take this opportunity to thank you for reading this Mills & Boon® book by offering you the chance to take FOUR more specially selected titles from the Medical™ series absolutely FREE! We're also making this offer to introduce you to the benefits of the Mills & Boon® Book Club—

- ★ **FREE home delivery**
- ★ **FREE gifts and competitions**
- ★ **FREE monthly Newsletter**
- ★ **Books available before they're in the shops**
- ★ **Exclusive Mills & Boon® Book Club offers**

Accepting these FREE books and gift places you under no obligation to buy; you may cancel at any time, even after receiving your free shipment. Simply complete your details below and return the entire page to the address below. You don't even need a stamp!

YES! Please send me 4 free Medical books and a surprise gift. I understand that unless you hear from me, I will receive 6 superb new titles every month for just £2.99 each, postage and packing free. I am under no obligation to purchase any books and may cancel my subscription at any time. The free books and gift will be mine to keep in any case.

M8ZEE

Ms/Mrs/Miss/Mr......................................Initials ....
BLOCK CAPITALS PLEASE

Surname ....

Address ....

....

....Postcode ....

Send this whole page to:
The Mills & Boon Book Club, FREEPOST CN81, Croydon, CR9 3WZ